DEDICATION

This collection is dedicated to all the independent writers and artists who work in relative obscurity.

Don't give up. Something good is coming.

Reflections in
Blue Water
and Other Stories

Richard Bist

CONTENTS

ACKNOWLEDGMENTS

No one who creates works solely in a vacuum. I want to acknowledge the encouragement and inspiration I've received from my teachers, my friends, and in a few cases, complete strangers on the internet.

A simple act of kindness can go a long way.

REFLECTIONS IN BLUE WATER

My wife, Maggie, never could tell a joke.

I was once again reminded of this fact while listening to her attempt to tell one at the Johnson's dinner party. We had already finished our four course exercise in overindulgence, during which numerous bottles of vintage wine were consumed. The guests were then ushered in to the fabled game room, complete with a cherry-wood pool table as the centerpiece and a Wurlitzer jukebox in the corner. Now the silk neckties were loosened and alabaster skin was flushing red under the light of Italian wall sconces.

Charles Campbell and I were throwing darts and sipping our well-aged Scotch when I overheard Maggie's voice rising above the din.

"Hush, hush," she slurred to the group standing around her, waving her hand as if it could mute sound. Her black satin dress was almost lost among the sea of designer evening wear, but I was able to pick her out of the crowd by the sparkling tiara that sat perched on top of her yellow curls. She paused long enough to take another sip of her Tom Collins, then snapped her fingers for attention. The conversation slowly died down, and when Maggie felt she had center stage, she began her long introduction to the joke.

I was just about to throw another dart when Charles elbowed me in the ribs. My shot went wide and the dart imbedded itself into the mahogany paneling.

"Hey Jon, don't you want to hear this?" he asked.

I sighed and shook my head. "Not really. She practiced on me all afternoon. Besides that, I lost my sense of humor about ten years ago."

"Ten years ago?" Charles mused, then it hit him. "Oh, you mean when you got married!"

That one sent him into peals of laughter, and he turned and stumbled over to join Maggie's audience.

I watched as the bodies pressed together around my wife, each clinging tightly to their drink of choice and leaning against one another for support. It seemed like this crowd drank in relation to their wealth. Only the finest imported wine and liquor would do. There would never be a six-pack of domestic beer in any of their refrigerators. That's why I was always a few drinks behind the rest of them. I felt out of place drinking from a bottle that cost more than I earned in a month, and I sure as hell wasn't going to use Maggie's family money to support my bad habits.

No one was paying attention to me as I slipped out through the French doors and into the backyard. The last thing I heard before I slid the door closed behind me was Maggie finishing her tale of where she heard the joke and how side-splittingly funny it was. I noticed that she glossed over the fact that she'd heard it from our maid. That wouldn't have been proper.

The night air was cool and refreshing and I was glad to get away from the haze of cigar smoke and heady perfumes. I walked along a garden path that wound its way through rows of rare flowers and manicured shrubs, a myriad of colors and shapes that even the dark couldn't suppress. I assumed a team of landscapers must have toiled for weeks to lay it all out, guys who earned their minimum wage baking under the South Florida sun and returned to their mobile homes at night to cool off with an oscillating fan and a six-pack of Old Milwaukee.

Eventually, the path brought me to the Johnson's swimming pool. It was a monstrosity of concrete and blue water. Olympic swim meets could have been held in this thing. It had to be close to fifty yards long, and about thirty wide. A diving board hung over the deep end, and in a tribute to bad taste, Bettie Johnson had a fountain placed right in the middle of the shallow end. The stone Cupid gave me a pleasant smile as I walked by. He didn't seem to mind me watching as he peed in the pool.

I've never actually seen the Johnson's swim, although I'm sure they paid some guy to come out and clean their pool every week. I don't know about Bettie's habits, but the only time I ever saw Fred Johnson get near water was when he splashed it into his Scotch.

As I walked along the hand-painted ceramic tile on the edge of the pool, I set my drink down on one of the patio tables and loosened my tie. Despite the night air, I was sweating. Probably the alcohol, although I usually don't get the sweats until the day after. I paused to remove my sport coat, then threw it and my tie over the back of a rod iron chair.

Looking at the dark, blue water of the pool, I remembered back to when Maggie and I were dating in college. We had cut out of her sorority party sometime around midnight and headed out to a pond that was just off campus. Not many people knew it was there, and that night Maggie had gotten it into her head that she wanted to go skinny dipping. Nothing I could say would dissuade her, and besides that, we were both young and drunk. I parked her car behind some brush so it couldn't be seen from the road, then we hurried through the woods to the water's edge.

It was a night not unlike this one. The sky was clear with a million stars twinkling above us, the moon a mere sliver. We were giggling and whispering as if someone might hear us while we stripped off our clothes amid the cover of the pine trees, then hand in hand we raced into the water. It was cold, and we both yelled out as we took the plunge. Shivering and covered in goose-bumps, we clung to one another for warmth. That night was the first time we made love, in the inky water, surrounded by the reflection of the universe.

I now stood on the diving board above the swimming pool, gazing at the stars reflected on the water's surface. That night at the pond seemed like only yesterday, but in my heart I knew it was so very long ago. Too much has happened since then. When we went back for our ten year reunion last month, the pond was gone, filled in and paved over for a parking lot. I think a part of me was buried there, as well.

The last time I saw the pond was on our wedding day. I stopped by there on my way to the church, although it was twenty miles out of my way. I needed to see it one last time before taking my vows. I wasn't nervous. I had no reason to be. Maggie's parents had refused to attend the wedding, so I didn't have to worry about them making a scene like they did on the night we announced our engagement. They didn't want to condone their daughter's marriage to someone outside their social standing. I couldn't care less. Despite what her parents said to anyone who would listen, I wasn't interested in her money, I was in love.

It was late morning when I finally made it to the end of the path and stood at the edge of the pond. I was trying to be careful and not get any mud on the patent leather dress shoes Maggie had bought me. It was the first pair I had ever owned. The pond looked different in the daylight. The water was still and smooth, like a polished gem. The surrounding pine trees were reflected on the surface, as was the cloudless sky, giving the water a blue sheen. This was the place where I had fallen in love, with fifteen dollars to my name and a pair of tennis shoes held together with duct tape. In another two hours I wouldn't have to want for anything ever again. Maggie would see to that.

And what would I be giving her in return? That was the question bothering me. Was it sex? Companionship? Or would it be something else, something less appealing? The men who ran in her parents circle were corporate types, CEO's and the like, and the women were submissive and supportive. Trophies. Maggie couldn't conform to that life, and with me on her arm she would never have to.

I picked up a stone and held it tightly in my hand as I gazed out on our pond, wishing I could go back in time. It was too late for that now. I threw the stone as hard as I could and watched as it hit the water with a splash. I had expected the surface to shatter like a mirror, but that didn't happen. The few ripples that formed were quick to disappear, and within a minute or two the surface of the pond was again smooth and unblemished.

With one last glance up at the night sky, I stepped off the diving board and felt the blue water envelop me, cold and sobering. I drifted downward until my shoes scraped the bottom of the pool. The only sounds were the soft hum of the filtration system and Cupid relieving himself in the shallow end. I stayed below the surface for as long as I could, my eyes closed tightly as I waited for something to happen. In my mind I could see Maggie smiling at me on our wedding day, her face alight with joy as she leaned in to kiss me.

Through the years that smile hadn't changed much. Maybe there were a few more wrinkles around the corners of her mouth, but that light was still there, and I had to wonder why I hadn't realized that before.

Finally, with my lungs burning, I pushed myself upwards until I surfaced and once again felt the night air on my face. I gasped for breath and looked around. From this angle the pool didn't appear quite as imposing as it did when I first saw it. Somehow it seemed smaller. I rolled onto my back and gently kicked my legs, propelling myself towards the steps in the shallow end as I admired the stars above me. They looked different, as well. Brighter, closer, more real. Or maybe it was the fact that I was looking at them from a different perspective.

I stepped out of the water and retrieved my coat and tie, poured the water out of my shoes, then made my way back to the house. I entered the game room just in time to hear Maggie deliver the punch line. As usual, her timing was off, and instead of a roar of laughter, all she received for her trouble was a few courtesy laughs and a number of groans. I waited by the door until the crowd broke up and slipped off into their usual groups before I crossed the room, my shoes still sloshing as I left a trail of chlorinated water in my wake. I passed Charles on the way and he asked if I wanted to finish our game. I told him I didn't think so. He started to turn away, but then paused and looked back at me.

"You look different," he commented, squinting his eyes. "Did you take off your glasses?"

"Yeah, that must be it," I replied. I didn't care to remind him that I never wore glasses. Charles laughed as he stumbled off. I shook my head and walked over to Maggie as she held reign over the far end of the bar.

"Honey! Where were you?" she asked as I approached her. "I needed you here for moral support."

"Oh, sorry. I needed some fresh air, so I stepped outside for a few minutes. Did I miss anything?"

She thought about this for a moment, then shook her head. "No, nothing really. Could you fix me another drink?"

"Sure," I said, taking her glass. As I turned she grabbed my arm. "Do you realize you're soaking wet?" she asked.

"Yeah," I replied. "Did you know there's a pool out back?"

Maggie nodded, then a big smile appeared on her face.

"Maybe we can go swimming later, like old times," she said.

"Yeah," I smiled in return. "Like old times."

COMPATIBILITY

The lunchroom was packed with disgruntled employees relishing their sixty-minutes of midday freedom. John stepped away from the lunch line cashier carrying his tray before him like a sacrificial offering. He strode through the maze of Formica tables and red plastic chairs, searching for an available seat. He spotted an empty table on the far side of the room and managed to make it there before anyone else. His closest neighbors were two middle-aged women sitting at a table several feet away, far enough to avoid interaction, but still close enough for him to eavesdrop.

After getting comfortable in front of his chicken salad sandwich and bowl of tomato soup, he tried to concentrate on the conversation taking place nearby. John had seen one of the women before. Her brilliant red hair had caught his attention several weeks ago when she first began working near him in the auditing department. It reminded him of his ex-wife's hair, that stunning red of an autumn sunset. They also had similar figures. John liked his women to have a little meat on their bones. It was just more to love, in his opinion. The woman worked several cubicles down from him, and although he had never actually met her, he was always aware of her comings and going.

He'd never seen the other woman before, although he assumed she worked in the building. She was a rail-thin brunette with too much makeup and grotesquely long fingernails that were painted black. John was familiar with her type. Loud and obnoxious, and usually found hanging out after work at the tavern next door.

The women appeared oblivious to his presence and made no attempt to lower their voices. John leaned in over his plate, grasping his sandwich firmly in both hands, and tried to concentrate on what they were saying over the background noise of the lunch room.

"I'm not sure if I should do it or not," the redhead moaned, dabbing her French fries in some ketchup. "I mean, I've been married to Brad for twenty years, and a part of me feels like I've put up with enough of his crap, you know? I deserve this. But another part of me feels guilty."

"About what?" the brunette asked as she helped herself to her companion's fries. "You haven't done anything yet."

"But I'm thinking about it."

"So what? Thinking about it isn't a crime. If it was, I'd be in trouble every time I saw a Chris Pratt movie."

They both laughed, causing John to jump a little in his seat. He stopped chewing momentarily, afraid that they'd noticed. When neither one of the women looked over he continued working on his chicken salad.

"Besides that," the brunette continued, "Randall is a helluva lot better looking than Brad. Live a little, that's all I'm saying."

"You think?"

"Sure. You only live once, honey, so you might as well enjoy yourself."

The redhead nodded as she ate her last fry. After a few more minutes of small talk, the brunette got up and headed back toward the offices. John finished his sandwich and pulled the bowl of Tomato soup closer, but when he looked down into the coagulating bowl of red liquid, he realized that he'd lost his appetite.

Out of the corner of his eye he could see the redhead sitting alone, running one finger aimlessly through the remnants of salt on her plate. The flaming red hair was like a halo of fire encircling her angelic face. John became suddenly aware of his heart beating in his chest, strong and loud. He was afraid that the redhead would hear it so he began taking slow, deep breaths in an attempt to slow it down, but to no avail. He knew what he was about to do, it was inevitable. And his hands were shaking.

He placed both hands on the table and stood, then picked up his tray and walked over to where the redhead was sitting. When he stopped beside her chair she looked up into his face, and to John's amazement, all his inhibitions melted away.

"Um, I wasn't trying to eavesdrop or anything," he said with a calm voice, "but I couldn't help but hear some of the conversation your were having with your friend. For what it's worth, I don't think you should do it. It wouldn't be right."

He turned before she could respond and hurried over to the trash bins to empty his tray. He felt electrified, empowered. It had been the first time he'd spoken to a woman in a non-professional manner since Barbara left him six months ago.

Sally licked the salt from her finger and watched the man walk away from her table. She had seen him around the office but hadn't been able to get him to speak to her, even though she made an effort to pass by his cubicle several times a day.

He appeared to be ex-military, just like her Brad, although this guy seemed to be holding up much better. She stared as he strode between the tables, his shoulders thrown back, chest extended, and the spine straight, just the way they teach it in basic training. It made the small hairs on the back of her neck stand up. He even sported a tattoo on his left forearm, an eagle with wings extended clasping a bunch of arrows in its talons. Sally thought it looked cool.

She waited until he had dumped his tray and left the cafeteria before getting up herself. She hadn't expected him to come over and speak to her like that. It had caught her off guard and left her grasping for something to say. Now she ran his words through her head, wondering how she could respond to them. She wasn't even sure if she should.

Once back inside the gray dullness of the auditing department, Sally passed through the rows of cubicles, pausing once to take a deep breath to calm her nerves. She walked up to where he sat and leaned in, but he had his back to her. She wasn't surprised to see that his cubicle was well organized. He even had framed photographs of the last three Republican presidents lined up along one wall. A small American flag hung from the bottom of each frame. On the corner of his desk sat a nameplate. Sally was glad she noticed it. It gave her an advantage.

"John?"

He jumped as if he'd been hit with an electric shock and spun around in his chair around to face her with wide eyes.

"Oh, it's you. I…"

"My name is Sally," she said and offered her hand.

John shook it firmly but gently. She liked the feel of his rough, dry palm.

"Listen, I wanted to thank you for what you said back there."

"You do? I mean, I thought I might have been out of line," John replied, his face reddening.

"No, not at all. In fact, I feel flattered that you took an interest in me. My husband, well, let's just say that things aren't what they used to be." Sally crossed her arms under her breasts, giving them a little lift. "We've sort of drifted. But I'm sure you and your wife..."

"I'm not married."

"Oh, really? I assumed a handsome man like yourself would have been snatched up a long time ago."

John eased back in his chair and sighed. "Actually, I was married. She left me some time ago. I haven't spoken about it much."

"I'm sorry to hear that," Sally said as she took a step closer to him. "Listen, would you like to maybe get together after work? We could have a few drinks and, you know, talk to each other. It might help us both."

A slow smile curled the corners of John's mouth. "Yeah, sure. Where would you like to meet?"

"Oh, let's just take my car," she replied, brushing a lock of her red hair back from her face. "It'll be easier that way."

Even back in the army, John had a hard time holding his liquor. One or two drinks were usually his limit, but Sally kept ordering more whiskey sours for him. He wasn't even sure what they had been talking about after a while. It had begun innocently enough, exchanging stories about their respective spouses, the trials and tribulations of marriage, the pain they had both experienced.

Then at some point the conversation veered off course. Sally's gaze became piercing, her soft, warm hand finding his cold, calloused one across the scarred wooden table. After another round of drinks she got up to use the restroom, and when she returned she sat down on his side of the booth. It wasn't long before her hand found his thigh.

He didn't remember who paid the bar tab or the ride home, but one thing was for certain, it was Sally's lips that pressed against his in the living room of his trailer. Her tongue slipped into his mouth as his heart pounded in his chest.

"So," she said, looking into his eyes as the moisture from their kiss glistened on her lips, "you never told me why your wife left."

"It's, well, it's a long story," John replied. He didn't want to get into it now, not at this moment.

"C'mon, don't be shy. You can tell me."

John ran his fingers through her hair and shook his head. "I, um…you know, some people have a hard time accepting things. Barbara didn't like certain things about me and, well, she dealt with it the best way she could."

"By leaving?" Sally asked as she began unbuttoning his shirt.

"Yeah, I guess so." John grabbed her wrists. "Listen, we shouldn't be doing this."

"Why not?"

"You're married."

"To a man I don't care about any more. You know what you said about accepting things? Well, Brad can't handle certain things about me either. I've tried to keep things exciting, but he's not willing to open his mind. We're just not compatible any more."

John looked down into Sally's blue eyes and his hands fell to his sides. "I want you."

"I know." Sally took him by the hand and led him down the hallway to his bedroom.

Resistance was the furthest thing from Johns mind as he stumbled down the dark hallway, past the plaques and framed commendations that lined the walls. It was all forgotten. The only thing that mattered now was this opportunity to somehow recapture what he had lost.

Bright rays of sunlight filtered in through the window blinds and warmed Sally's face, eventually drawing her out of her dreams. She held up a hand to block the light and glanced at the alarm clock on the dresser. It was seven o'clock, earlier than she usually awoke on Saturdays. She moaned and rolled over, expecting to spoon up behind John, but his side of the bed was empty. She sat up, rubbing her eyes, and noticed that the light was on in the bathroom.

Throwing the covers back, she walked as quietly as she could across the bedroom floor, the cool morning air raising goose bumps on her naked flesh. The bathroom door was slightly ajar, and she leaned in to see what John was up to. As soon as she did, however, she had to clasp a hand over her mouth to keep from crying out.

John was standing in front of the bathroom mirror attempting to hook the clasp of Sally's bra behind his back. He had already slipped on her panties, and they hugged his buttocks like a second skin. It took several tries, but he finally succeeded in securing the bra. He then snapped to attention, feet planted firmly and his arms at his sides. He stood rigid for a moment, then snapped a formal salute to himself.

Sally couldn't believe her eyes. Without a word she pushed the door open and walked up behind John, wrapping her arms around him tightly. He jumped and tried to pull away, but she wouldn't let him.

"I can explain…," he stammered.

"Don't bother," Sally said as she leaned her face against his warm back. "I understand, probably more than you realize. Remember when I said I had tried to add some excitement to my marriage?"

John nodded and turned to face her. "So you're okay with this?"

"Yes, I am."

John pulled her to him and held her tightly. "I don't know what to say."

"Don't say anything," she replied. "Just do me one favor."

"Anything," John whispered.

"Please don't stretch out my good lingerie."

"You've got it," he said, and he buried his face in her long red hair.

DIRTY LAUNDRY

It was a few minutes after midnight when I entered the Laundromat. I had been working there for only two weeks, but already the industrial gray walls and smell of bleach were becoming too familiar. It took a moment for my eyes to adjust to the glaring fluorescent lights, but once they did I noticed Larry, the owner of the Suds-O-Rama, sitting behind the counter like forgotten royalty. His massive bulk was perched atop a far too fragile bar stool. Each time he shifted his weight I expected the creaking wooden legs to explode in a shower of splinters. It hadn't happened yet, but I figured it would be soon. He looked up from his ledger as I made my way across the stained linoleum tiles.

"Damn, Sean, where the hell have you been? I thought you were gonna be a no-show."

"Sorry," I replied as I tossed my notebook on the counter. "I dozed off watching The Tonight Show…"

"That new guy they got hosting ain't shit compared to Carson."

Larry stood up, grabbed my notebook and began thumbing through the pages with a frown on his face.

"So how's the Great American Writer coming along?" he asked. "This doesn't look like much more than a bunch of crap. What's this here? He slipped into his dark depression like a comfortable pair of pants…"

"Give me that," I said, snatching the tattered pages out of his hands. "I'm still working on some ideas, you know, looking for inspiration. The words will come when they're ready…"

"That bullshit again?" Larry snorted as he moved from behind the counter. "I still don't understand why you think you can find inspiration sitting in a laundromat in the middle of the night. You know, for a rich kid, you ain't too bright."

I took my place behind the counter and eased myself onto the unpleasantly warm bar stool.

"Listen…," I began, but Larry was on a roll.

"No, seriously. You went to all those fancy private schools, right? And what's that got ya'? Zilch. You shoulda done what I did and run away from home at fourteen. Hell, look at me. I own my own business, my own house, and I got stories that'll put some hair on that bird chest of yours."

"Yeah, yeah, I know all about your stories, but I want to write about something meaningful, not those disgusting donkey shows you saw in Tijuana."

Larry shook his head. "Hey, the only way you're gonna get any inspiration is from experience, not hiding out in here…"

"Where I don't have any distractions…"

"Whatever," he said, throwing his hands in the air. "You don't know nothin', kid. I'm outta here. The dryer loads should be done around two a.m. or so, then switch over the stuff from washers two and five. I'll see you in the morning."

I watched as Larry waddled out to the parking lot and squeezed into the gleaming red 1979 Cadillac that was his pride and joy. The car sagged visibly as he settled in behind the wheel and a minute later he pulled out onto the empty street. As I saw his taillights slip away into the darkness I remembered a dream I'd had the night before. I saw myself walking into the Laundromat wearing a sports coat and slacks, a hardback book tucked under my arm. I marched up to the counter where Larry was sitting, but before he could say anything I smacked him as hard as I could across the head with the book. After he fell to the floor, I tossed the book on the counter and that's when I saw the cover. It read, "The Great American Novel by Sean Easton."

But I knew it was still a pipe-dream. At the rate I was going, I would be working for Larry for the next ten years. I shook my head to chase off the remnants of the dream, then opened my notebook and began searching for my Muse.

I must have zoned out for a while because I never heard the buzzers when the dryers finished their cycles. Or maybe it was that

I just didn't care. Either way, I was still struggling over the pages of my notebook hours later, writing and rewriting, trying to find the spark I needed to make the words all come together. I could picture the ideas in my head, piece them together in a way that made sense and sounded right, but when I got it down on paper it just looked like crap.

Maybe Larry was right, maybe I didn't have whatever it was that I needed to be a writer, or at least a good writer. I was beginning to think I would have to settle with being a hack, penning erotic letters for some men's magazine, or writing nauseating verse for a greeting card company. Or in the worse case scenario, I would have to swallow my pride and go home. My parents would be more than happy to take me back into the nest, but I wasn't ready to give up just yet.

I had just scratched out another line and was trying to reword it when a shadow crossed the page. It startled me that I hadn't heard anyone walk in. When I looked up to greet my late-night customer I almost fell off the stool.

The guy standing on the other side of the counter was covered with blood. It was all over the front of his t-shirt and jeans, and some had splattered up on his neck and arms. At first I froze. I didn't know if the guy had been shot or something, and to be honest, I didn't know what to think. I just stood there waiting for him to speak or drop dead. After a moment he raised his eyebrows and asked if there was a problem.

"Ah, no man," I stammered, "you just, um, caught me by surprise."

"Think you can give me change for this?" he asked, showing me the five-spot he was holding.

"Yeah, sure. You, ah, want quarters, right?"

"If that's what these machines take."

My hands were shaking pretty bad as I tried to key open the register. Once I got the drawer open I fumbled with the loose change, spilling some on the floor as I tried to count out twenty quarters.

"You nervous or something?" the guy asked, looking at my trembling hands.

"No, just too much caffeine, I guess." I tried to say it with a laugh, but all that came out was a muffled croak.

"You should cut back. That stuff'll kill you."

He scooped the change off the counter with blood-stained

hands and walked over to the row of vending machines against the far wall. As soon as his back was turned I sat back on my stool and tried to figure out what to do, but before I could gather my thoughts I heard the guy say something. I looked up at him with my mouth hanging open and tried to comprehend the words coming out of his mouth. He stared at me for a moment, then snapped his fingers a few times, like a hypnotist waking their subject at the end of their session.

"I asked which of these detergents is best for getting out stains like this."

"Try the green box," I replied.

I watched him pump his quarters into the machine and make his selection. After retrieving his laundry soap and buying a soda, he walked to the back of the Laundromat. He stopped in front of the last machine and proceeded to strip. I picked up my pen and pretended to write, but out of the corner of my eye I watched as he carefully removed each article of clothing and dropped them in the washing machine. A box of detergent, a handful of quarters, and the soft rumbling of the old machine soon filled the air. Clad in only his boxers, the guy disappeared into the restroom.

Alone for the moment, I took the time to try to figure out what I was supposed to do. My hand instinctively went for the phone, but I hesitated before making contact. Who would I call? The cops? Yeah, officer, I've got a bloody guy doing laundry here, you wanna come pick him up? Even if I called and the cops came, what happens then? The guy could come out of the restroom and catch me on the phone, or worse yet, see the cops pull up and use me as a hostage or something.

Before I could come to a decision the guy stepped out of the restroom drying his hands with a paper towel. Without the blood he looked pretty normal, and to my great relief, less threatening. If I had to guess, I would have said he wasn't much older than me, although the creases on his sun-darkened face told another story. His blond hair was short-cropped and he sported a rose tattoo on his right bicep. He seemed unconcerned with me as he sat down on a metal folding chair near the back of the room and picked up a tattered copy of Good Housekeeping, thumbing through the pages until he found something of interest.

I could tell by the sound that the washer had finished the first cycle and was refilling for the rinse, so I knew it would be awhile before the clothes were ready for the dryer. I figured I might as well do something constructive and grabbed a broom.

As I swept the floor I tried to keep an eye on the guy without being obvious, but I don't think he really cared what I was doing. He just sat there sipping his drink and flipping through the magazines. I soon found myself sweeping closer to where he sat. When the final buzzer went off on the washer I was standing right next to it, and I nearly wet my pants. I moved aside and watched as the guy pulled his wet clothes out of the machine.

"It doesn't look like that detergent worked very well," he said as he inspected his damp clothes.

"Yeah, blood...um, blood stains can be a pain. You could try running the load again on cold water and see if that helps."

"Thanks."

I felt like an idiot standing there watching the guy do his laundry, but I couldn't help myself. A dozen questions formed in my mind, things I wanted to ask him. Luckily, he decided to break the ice.

With the washer humming, he sat back in the chair and looked up at me.

"I can tell you're pretty uncomfortable with this, and I don't blame you. As soon as my stuff is done I'll be out of your hair."

"No problem," I replied, but I continued to stand there, unsure of how to proceed.

An uncomfortable silence followed, and a few heartbeats later the guy sighed and tossed his magazine aside.

"I'm sorry if I freaked you out, but I really need to get cleaned up. Blood-stained clothes have a way of drawing attention, you know?"

I nodded like an idiot and wondered if he was finally going to get fed up with me and do something unpleasant. That's when it occurred to me that it might be better to appear sympathetic and stay on his good side.

"So what happened? I mean, with the blood and all."

The smile disappeared from his face and I thought I had gone too far, but he just sighed and shook his head.

"What happened tonight was a long time coming. I'm sure you guessed from the condition I was in, the blood . . .," he trailed off.

For the next few minutes the only sound in the place was the soft chugging of the washer. Something in the back of my mind told me to keep pressing, keep him talking. I didn't want him to feel that I was a threat.

"Was it an accident?" I asked.

The guy laughed, but it had a hollow sound.

"No, it wasn't an accident. I knew what I was doing, I'd never deny that. What happened was unavoidable."

"But what happened? Was it self-defense? You know, if it was it's not like you'd get in trouble or anything..."

"It doesn't matter, not anymore," he said, then took a sip of his soda. "You're not from around here, are you?"

I leaned against the washer, trying to appear casual. "No, I grew up in a small town in Oklahoma. Why?"

"Mmm, I figured as much. Small town folks, they know what's going on with everyone else, they know each other's dirty laundry...no secrets, right?"

I nodded.

"But people in the city," he continued, "hell, they just don't care. You have to take care of yourself."

"Oh, come on. That's bull."

"Is it? How old are you? Eighteen? Nineteen?"

"Yeah, I'm eighteen."

He shook his head. "Man, you just don't know...This ain't the Midwest, and you definitely aren't in Kansas anymore..."

"Oklahoma," I corrected him.

"Whatever. Just remember, kid, you've got to look out for yourself..."

He trailed off and looked out the front window. I turned around in time to see a car pulling up out front. The glass had frosted up from the humidity, so it was hard to tell who it was. When I looked back at him I saw that his face had hardened.

"Why don't you go hang out in the restroom for a few minutes," I offered.

The guy gave me a look that let me know that this was no time to screw around, then he got up and slipped through the bathroom door. I picked up my broom and had just made it to the front counter when a guy with starched jeans and a black leather jacket walked in. He had the deviated septum and scarred face of someone who had made a career out of violence, and his hair was slicked back like some television mobster. There was also a very obvious bulge under his left arm. He paused near the door to take a quick look around the place, then walked over to the counter.

"How's it going tonight? Can I help you with something?" I

asked, trying to keep the fear out of my voice. I kept my hands beneath the counter so he couldn't see them trembling.

"Yeah, yeah, maybe you can," he replied as he looked me over with his bloodshot eyes. "I'm lookin' for a guy...uh, how do I put this? He's, uh, in his early twenties, blond hair, about five-ten or so, and he's probably got some, uh, blood on him."

"Blood?" I said with wide eyes. "Jesus. No, man, I haven't seen anyone like that."

"You sure? I thought I saw someone in the back wid' you when I pulled up."

My hands were shaking uncontrollably now, but I tried not to think about that. Instead, I bit the inside of my cheek. The instant of pain kept me focused on what I was doing.

"Oh, that was probably just a reflection off the front window..."

"So you wouldn't mind if I took a look around that place?"

My mind was racing, but that was when inspiration kicked in.

"Actually, I would. One of the toilets overflowed on me and there's shit all over the floor back there. If it's that important to you, you're welcome to stick your head in back there, but I wouldn't recommend it."

The guy winced and shook his head.

"No, that's okay," he said. He looked at his watch, then back at me. "Listen, the guy I'm lookin' for is named Clint, and it's very important that I find him. Anyone comes in here matchin' that description I gave you, give me a call. There could be a reward in it for you."

I flinched as he reached into his jacket, and he smiled as he pulled out a business card and handed it to me. It was blank except for a phone number printed across one side.

"So, are you a cop or something?" I asked.

"Let's just say I work outside the law," he said as his smiled widened, exposing two gold teeth, "so you don't need to tell the cops about this. You see this guy, you call me, and I'll take care of ya'."

The guy rapped the countertop with his scarred knuckles, then turned and left. I waited until his car pulled out of the lot before trying to stand. My knees felt like all the strength had been sapped out of them, and the palms of my hands had little red half-moons in them from where my fingernails had dug in. It took a few minutes for me to regain my composure enough to walk to the back and let Clint know that it was safe to come out of the restroom.

"I don't know why you did that," he said as we shook hands, "but thanks."

I just shrugged my shoulders. I didn't know why either, and I really didn't know what else to say. In the awkward moment that followed I glanced up at the clock on the wall.

"It's almost three-thirty. You should probably get going before daybreak."

Clint nodded, then turned to the washer.

"Yeah, but my clothes…"

"Here, take these," I said, pulling some sweatpants and a t-shirt out of one of the large hampers nearby. Clint dressed and we walked to the front door.

"Good luck," I said.

He looked at me and smiled, then opened the door and stepped into the night.

I didn't notice when morning arrived. After Clint left I sat down behind the counter, picked up my pen and started writing. The words came slow at first, but they gradually began to pick up speed, and before I knew it I was in the zone, writing as I'd never done before. My experience that night did something to me, kicked in something dormant that had been hiding within my mind. Maybe it was the fear or adrenaline. Maybe it was because I finally got to experience life like I never had before.

I also didn't notice when Larry came in at seven a.m. to relieve me. I don't know how long he stood in front of the counter before slamming his hand down on it. Although I heard it, I barely flinched. My mind was elsewhere. I finished the paragraph I was working on and dropped my pen in relief. My fingers were beginning to cramp.

"Damn, boy, what's gotten into you?" Larry asked as he unwrapped his breakfast burrito and took a bite.

I shrugged. "Inspiration. I guess my Muse finally decided to pay a visit."

Larry frowned as he chewed. While he processed this new information, I grabbed my pen and notebook and slipped out from behind the counter.

"Well, your shift's over, so get the hell out of here. Oh, and don't be late tonight or I'll have to dock your pay."

I started walking towards the door, then stopped and turned.

"I'll do you one better," I said. "I quit."

Larry almost choked. He took a quick swallow of soda and wiped his mouth.

"What? Quit? Boy, you've lost your damn mind."

"Maybe so, but I'm tired of doing other people's dirty laundry. It's time I lived my life."

"So what are you gonna do? Write for a living?" he asked with a smirk.

I turned my head and looked out the front window. The sun was just beginning to rise beyond the concrete skyline and its first rays caressed my face like a warm breath.

"Yeah, I think I will," I replied. "And you know what, Larry? As soon as my first book is published, I'll be sure to bring you an autographed copy."

I almost laughed when his mouth dropped open, but instead I saluted him and walked outside to greet the new day.

A SPRING MOURNING

It was a bright April afternoon and the boy was sitting on the porch counting the cars that lined the street in front of his house. With so many visitors it would be easy to assume that it was some sort of happy occasion, like his fourth birthday party a few months ago. Instead everyone was wearing dark clothing and somber expressions. To make matters worse, he was the only child in attendance, which meant that he was stuck with only his imagination for company.

The mood inside the house had become too much for him to bear, so he had retreated to a sunny spot on the porch to enjoy the fresh air. He had only been sitting for a few minutes when a man and woman came walking up from the street. They were also dressed in black and the boy could tell by the woman's red and watery eyes that she had recently been crying. As they approached, the man handed his wife a handkerchief and put an arm around her shoulders, then asked the boy if his father was available. Grudgingly the boy rose from his place in the sunlight and reentered the gloomy interior of the house.

Once inside, he began to scan the crowd for his father, but he was having a hard time spotting him in the sea of faces. As he made his way across the room people began to reach for him, squeezing his shoulders and wrapping him in unwanted embraces. Tears from the faces of strangers were collecting on his shirt and matting his hair, and the pitiful looks were beginning to frighten him.

He finally made it to the hallway and decided to check the bedrooms for his father. The first door he came to was his own, and he peeked inside to make sure none of his things had been disturbed. Although he had made his bed, toys were still strewn across the floor. Many of them were presents he had received for his birthday, but lately he had lost interest in playing with them. Probably because his mother wasn't there to join in the fun. With a sigh he closed the door and continued down the hall.

The next door he came to, his parents, was closed, but he could hear muted whispers through the wood. He reached for the knob, then slowly opened the door. He had found his father. He and a family friend, Mr. Campice, were sitting on the edge of the bed. The boy's father had his face buried in his hands while Mr. Campice, with an arm around the man's shoulders, spoke sympathetic words to him.

The boy turned to leave, but he stopped when he heard his father call to him. He quickly ran across the room to his father's embrace, wrapping his arms around the man's neck and hanging on as tightly as he could. After a moment the boy began to sense that something was wrong. He stepped back from his father and felt a blow to his heart. He had never seen his father in pain before, had never seen him cry, but his face at that moment would forever be burned in the boy's memory. It had seemingly changed overnight from that of a healthy and happy middle-aged man to that of someone twice his age.

The worst part was his eyes; they were no longer the gentle, loving eyes of his father. No, these were now the eyes of despair. The boy was in shock, unable to grasp what had happened to his father. He stumbled backward, then turned and ran out of the room. He could feel himself beginning to lose control. His mind was a jumbled mess that was slowly growing numb. Frantically, he fought his way against the tangle of arms and legs, finally making it to the front door and back into the sunlight.

Outside the scene hadn't changed; the sun was still shining, the sky still clear and blue. The boy stood on the porch for a few minutes to clear his head, then went around the side of the house and let himself through the gate into the back yard. As he stopped to pet his dogs he heard the familiar squeaking of the swing-set and wondered who would be back there. He peeked around the corner and saw a young woman wearing a white dress and wide-brimmed hat slowly swaying back and forth. She seemed so out of place at such a somber gathering, yet she also seemed to fit so naturally with the surrounding day.

After a while the woman seemed to sense the boy's presence. She turned to look at him and motioned for him to come join her. Avoiding eye contact, he walked over and climbed into the empty swing next to her. They sat in silence for a bit, just floating back and forth and enjoying the day. Birds were singing in the trees, a dog barked, and someone's laughter filtered over from the next street.

Everything seemed peaceful again. His head had finally cleared and the episode in the house was fading like a bad dream. The woman still hadn't spoken and the boy felt an aversion to looking directly at her. Instead, he tried to steal a few quick glances at her when he thought she couldn't see him. Time passed slowly, and finally the woman broke the silence.

"Do you know why so many people are at your house?" she asked.

"Sort of," the boy replied. "My mom went away, I mean passed away, and all these people came over."

The woman smiled. "That's right, these people are friends of your parents. They've all gotten together to support your father through these rough times."

"What do you mean?"

"Well, your mother has gone to be with the angels and your father is upset by that. It hurts him inside because he loves her and misses her."

"But isn't it good to be with the angels?"

"Yes, it is," the woman answered, "it's wonderful."

"Then why is everyone so sad?"

Once again the woman smiled. "They're sad because they are going to miss her. They all cared for her very much."

They were silent for a few minutes as the boy processed this new information, then more questions occurred to him.

"Should I be sad, too?" he asked.

"Yes, but only if you feel the need to be." She looked up at the sky. "Of course, it is a beautiful day and I would hate to see you cry."

"Do you think my mom is sad?"

"She was at first," the woman replied, "but that was because she didn't want to leave any of you. She's okay now. She knows your father will find someone to help him forget his pain, and the both of you will be happy."

"How does she know?"

"She just does."

"Oh."

They fell silent again. A mockingbird in a nearby tree scolded a sparrow that flew too close.

"Will I ever see my mom again?" the boy asked.

The woman didn't seem to expect this question and stopped swinging for a moment. The boy felt a chill run through his body as a cloud obscured the sun, but it quickly passed.

The woman sighed and said, "Yes, you will see her again, but not for a long time. You shouldn't worry, though, because she will always be with you, watching over you and protecting you."

"I'm glad," the boy said with a smile, "I knew she would never really go away."

The boy stopped swinging as the woman rose and stood before him. The sun was just behind her head, and to the boy it looked as if she was wrapped in a golden glow.

"Are you leaving now?" the boy asked, although he already knew the answer.

"Yes, I must go."

"I wish you didn't. I like talking with you."

"I wish I could stay, too. I also wish we could have gotten to know each other better, but it wasn't meant to be." She reached down and brushed some hair back from his brow. "Don't be sad, though, because we will see each other again someday, and then we'll have all the time in the world."

"I'd like that," the boy said.

"Well, you must close your eyes now."

"Okay."

The woman leaned down and gently kissed the boy's forehead, and when he opened his eyes she was gone.

A GAME OF CHESS

Maria stepped into the study carrying a tray laden with a coffee urn and three cups. Her husband and his childhood friend, Antonio, sat at a small table near the window, smoking hand-rolled cigarettes as their voices filled the room. Maria did not want to interrupt their conversation. She had other things on her mind, and the thoughts distracted her as she unburdened the tray and placed its contents on the large oaken desk. The smell of the coffee roused the men and they came over to join her.

"Do you see, Antonio? Even after all these years together, she stills treats me like a king."

Maria turned to the men, the look on her face stifling their laughter, although their grins still remained.

"Yes, Antonio, I still treat him well, but it is only because he will whine like un niño if he does not get his way. Isn't that so, dear husband?"

"A child?" Frederick replied. "Behave yourself, woman. Antonio will not believe your lies."

Antonio laughed. "You forget, mi amigo, she and I know you better than that."

Frederick shook his hands at the ceiling in mock exasperation, then gave his wife a wink.

"Bah, I should know better than to allow you both to be in the same room together. You conspire to ruin me." He slapped Antonio on the arm, then kissed Maria's cheek as she handed him a cup of coffee. "Now, let us sit and relax. We have a long day ahead of us."

"A long day for you, perhaps. I plan on taking care of business early, then asking your wife to go horseback riding," Antonio stated.

"Riding? That sounds like a good idea. It will help you to relax after your humiliating defeat, don't you agree, dear?" He turned to his wife and saw her staring into the distance. "What is the matter, my love? Are you not feeling well?"

Maria looked up with a start. "I'm sorry. I'm fine. It's just that..."

"What is it, Maria?" Antonio asked. "We are all friends here."

"I'm worried about the children."

The two men looked at one another in puzzlement.

"What of them?" Frederick asked.

"Well, they have never met, and they are both at that age..."

Frederick smiled. "Maria, they will be fine. They are no longer children. They are young adults now, and we cannot worry about imaginings."

Maria looked guiltily at Antonio, then spoke. "I'm concerned about Isabella. I know that Cristo is a young man, and young men have urges. I'm not so old that I cannot remember having to fight off many . . ."

She was interrupted by the laughter of the men.

"Oh, my dear, I must tell you that your fears are unfounded," Fredrick said. "I don't think that Antonio's son is going to corrupt our daughter. Cristo is a shy and reserved young man, and I do not believe he will damage Isabella in any way. Am I right, my friend?"

Antonio nodded. "Yes, you can put aside your fears. Cristo has shown an interest in women, but I am still trying to help him overcome his shyness. That is why your husband and I thought it would be good for him to come with me this time. He does not get out of our city very often, so we thought that spending the day with Isabella would help draw him out of his shell."

"But do you think it's a good idea to leave them alone?" Maria persisted.

Frederick smiled and patted his wife's hand. "Not to worry, dear. From what Antonio tells me, Cristo is very adept at dodging the advances of amorous women. The honor of our daughter is safe. Besides, Isabella will be going to St. Teresa's in a few weeks. Her religious studies are foremost in her mind." He pushed himself back from the desk and stood. "So, now that the pleasantries are over, shall we begin?"

Antonio poured another cup of coffee and smiled. "Are you so eager to be defeated, my friend?"

"Oh, no! I am eager to meet such a worthy opponent on the battle field. I am ready to wage war!"

"War? How many times do I have to tell you, Frederick? Chess is not a game of blood and sweat. It is a subtle test of strategy and finesse, of paciencia y la seducción."

Frederick laughed loudly. "Did you hear that, Maria? Our amigo is ever the romantic. Come now, oh brave Antonio, let us see if you can seduce me!"

Both men laughed as they sat down at the table near the window. The morning sun was shining in through the glass and lit the ivory board with a bright flame, highlighting the hand-carved ivory chess pieces. Maria remained at the desk with her thoughts and watched the men as they studied the board. Even though they had tried to soothe her fears, she still felt a gnawing suspicion in the pit of her stomach. It was true that Isabella and Cristo were no longer children and it probably would be good for them to spend some time together. But this was the last summer at home for both of them, which only added to Maria's unease.

She took a sip of coffee and watched as the men began to study the board. How many years had they been playing this game? Too many to count. She had given the household staff the day off so the men wouldn't be disturbed and planned to wait on them herself. It was her gift to her husband.

After a few minutes of planning, the first pawns were moved and the match began. Her husband's strong, brown fingers moved with abrupt precision, grasping each piece firmly as his strategy unfolded. He preferred to come at his opponents directly. Antonio, by contrast, had thin, subtle fingers, and his strategy was to slowly wear down his opponent with finesse. In her mind, it was almost like watching a ballet as their hands moved back and forth, twisting and turning to some unheard orchestra.

The sunlight glaring off the pool water momentarily blinded Cristo as he stepped through the French doors and out onto the sprawling back patio. His father had told him to come out here to meet Isabella, and Cristo had reluctantly agreed, but he would rather have been inside watching the chess match.

As he neared the pool he wiped his sweaty palms against his

trousers and tried to fight the queasy feeling in his stomach. He had no idea what to expect from this girl. His father had said she was attractive but kept sheltered by her father, which is probably why he arranged for them to meet. It was almost time for both of them to leave home for the first time. Cristo tried to bolster his courage by rationalizing that a little social interaction would be good before stepping out into the world.

"Hola."

The voice brought him out of his thoughts, and he looked down into the clear blue water to see a beautiful young woman gazing up at him.

"I was wondering when you were going to get here," she said. "The brushes and other equipment are in the tool shed. I'll be out of the pool in a few minutes, then you can get started."

The young woman continued swimming to the far end of the pool, then turned and saw him standing with a dumbfounded look on his face.

"I must say, I find it very rude when a man stares like that. You're being paid to clean the pool, not gawk at me."

Realization sunk in and Cristo smiled.

"I sorry, but I'm not here to clean your pool. My name is Cristo, I'm Antonio's son. I assume you're Isabella?"

"Well, why didn't you say so. Yes, I'm Isabella. Why don't you sit under the umbrella over there and cool off. You must be terribly warm in those long pants. I'll be done in a few minutes."

Before Cristo could reply, the beautiful face disappeared under the water. He shrugged his shoulders and sat down at a white iron table shaded by a large white umbrella. Isabella had already reached the near end of the pool and was now swimming back to the far side. He tried not to stare at her sleek form gliding through the water like some soft, bronze mermaid.

He was attempting to admire the surrounding landscaping when she stepped out of the water, and he didn't realize that she was standing beside him until she spoke.

"You have your father's good looks."

Cristo turned his head to reply, but found he was at a loss for words. Isabella stood before him in her swimsuit, her skin browned by the sun and beaded with water. A knowing smile played on her lips as she saw his reaction.

Remembering his manners, Cristo attempted to stand, but Isabella put a hand on his shoulder and sat in the chair across from him. Cristo was doing his best look her in the eyes.

"So what shall we do to keep ourselves occupied while our fathers play their game? Maybe we should play a game as well. What do you think?" the young woman asked.

Cristo wiped the sweat from his forehead and shrugged. "This is your house, so I guess I will leave it to you to decide."

Isabella leaned towards him as a few drops of water fell from her chin and landed on his knee.

"Oh, I can think of quite a few things we could do together," she said while brushing at the wet spots on his leg.

Cristo crossed his legs and attempted to change the subject. "I, uh, see that your family has a stable. Perhaps we can go horseback riding."

The smile faded on Isabella's face, but only for a moment. She stood and grabbed her towel. "Very well, we'll go riding. But I get to pick what we do after that. Now let's go in so I can put on something more appropriate, then we'll go have some fun."

"You go ahead, I'll be in shortly," Cristo replied. The girl turned and started towards the house as he sat back in his chair and took a deep breath. His father had understated her beauty, probably on purpose. He again wiped the sweat from his brow, then stood and walked toward the shade of the house. It would probably be a good idea for him to change his clothes as well. The heat was almost unbearable.

The room was quiet. The two men sat at the small table, faces set with furrowed brows as each contemplated the chess board. Moves had been made, pieces taken, but the outcome was far from obvious. They had already lost track of real time, their attention focused solely on the game pieces that represented their armies at war.

They had also forgotten the presence of the quiet woman who sat across the room, although she too was lost in thought. Despite Frederick and Antonio's attempt to allay her fears, Maria was still worrying about the children being left alone together.

The grandfather clock in the corner tolled the half-hour and stirred Maria from her thoughts. The men would be breaking soon to eat and relax and she needed to prepare their meal. She would also take the opportunity to check on Isabella and see if she was behaving herself. Eager to be on her way, Maria stood and quietly walked over to see how the match was proceeding.

Having decided on a move, Frederick stirred. "Pawn takes bishop."

Antonio grimaced, thought for a moment, then countered. "Pawn to queen's rook three."

"Bishop takes knight. Check."

Maria saw a grin of satisfaction spread on Frederick's face.

"Pawn takes bishop," was Antonio's response. He had easily saved his king, but that did not matter. Frederick had gone for an early check as a way of drawing first blood and rattling his opponent, putting him on an early defensive. It was merely a skirmish. The war itself was far from over.

Back inside the house, Cristo figured that he had a few minutes to change his clothes while Isabella was dressing, so he headed for the guest room that he was sharing with his father. As he entered the bedroom, he pulled off his sweat-soaked shirt and trousers and hung them over a chair, then proceeded to rummage through his bags in search of more appropriate clothes.

When he heard the soft click of the door closing behind him, he thought is was his father taking a break from the chess match, but the voice that spoke made his heart stop.

"Is there anything I can help you with?"

He spun around in alarm, grabbing at the nearest available piece of clothing to cover himself with. Isabella stood with her back against the door, her lips pulled up in a wicked smile.

"What are you doing in here?" Cristo asked.

"Just checking to see if you needed any help getting ready, but I can see you've already chosen your riding outfit," Isabella replied, her eyes glancing downward. "I like your choice, but it may be a bit understated."

Cristo looked down to see that he was covering himself with a sock. He felt the blood rush to his face and quickly grabbed a pillow off the nearby bed. When he looked up, Isabella was slowly crossing the room towards him. He tried to back away, but the bed blocked his escape. The butterflies were again stirring in his stomach, and there was also an undeniable stirring beneath the pillow he was holding.

"You shouldn't be in here, it isn't right..."

Isabella stopped directly in front of him and put a soft finger against his lips. "Shh, Cristo. No one needs to know about this. Our parents are busy downstairs and the servants have all been sent away for the day. Besides, we are both adults now." She removed her finger from his lips and slid her hand down to his bare chest.

"Your heart is beating so fast," she said with a whisper, leaning in closer until their lips were almost touching. Cristo felt as if he was out of control. His head was swimming and the pressure below his waist was almost unbearable. He was ready to forget about remaining chaste when there was a knock at the door.

"Isabella? Cristo? Are either of you in there?"

"My mother," Isabella sighed. She gave Cristo a quick kiss on the lips, then dropped to the floor and slid under the bed. Cristo stood for a moment, unsure of what to do, then scurried to the door and opened it enough to peek into the hall.

"I am in here, señora, alone, changing clothes. Isabella is not here. I haven't seen her," he said, then closed the door before Maria could reply. He walked back to the bed to grab some clothing, then strode to the bathroom.

"I am going to get dressed," he announced.

"Can I help?" asked the voice from under the bed.

Cristo did not reply, but he locked the bathroom door, just in case.

The men were sitting on the patio smoking cigarettes and discussing horse breeding when Maria came out to join them. She frowned when she saw they were flicking their ashes onto the crumb-covered plates.

"Ah, my dear," Frederick said as his wife sat down, "my thanks for a wonderful snack. Battle always makes for a hearty appetite. Do you agree, Antonio?"

Sitting across the table, Antonio merely smiled and patted his belly.

Frederick turned back to his wife and asked, "And where have you been? Checking on our children, I suppose."

"If you must know, then yes, I was checking on them. Well, at least I found Cristo. He was in his room changing clothes. I couldn't find our daughter anywhere."

"She is probably down at the stables."

"Or," Antonio began, "maybe she was hiding on the window ledge when you looked in on Cristo."

Frederick laughed, but Maria did not. She gave both men a disapproving look.

"Antonio, I am surprised at you," she stated, "I expect better manners from my guests."

"You are right, Maria, and I apologize if I offended you. I spoke in jest. Will you still accompany me this afternoon for our horseback ride?"

"I suppose," she sighed, "but that will all depend on how late it is when you two are finished."

"Not to worry," Frederick said, "it won't take me long to break through Antonio's defenses."

"Is that what you think?" Antonio asked. "I am only just beginning to pick your strategy apart, my friend. I can ward off any attack you may throw at me."

"Very well. Let us return to the study and finish our match."

The men rose and returned to the house. Maria pulled a cigarette from the pack her husband had left on the table. She usually didn't smoke and had a hard time getting a flame from the lighter, but she prevailed and soon her head was swimming from the nicotine.

After a few minutes it passed and she began to relax. The chess game was going to be all consuming for the next several hours, so she wouldn't be able to wander far from the room in case they needed anything. That meant several hours that Isabella and Cristo would be alone together. It made her uncomfortable and she wasn't sure why.

She crushed out the half-smoked cigarette in an ashtray and returned to the study. The men had already resumed their match and seemed oblivious to her presence, so she decided to sit in a chair closer to the chessboard to better watch the play. The men had obviously been thinking of strategy during lunch because they were quickly performing a series of moves. For a few minutes no pieces were taken. Instead, they were vying for position. Then the skirmish began.

"Bishop takes pawn," Frederick announced.

"Bishop to king-three," was Antonio's counter.

"Queen takes pawn."

"Queen to queen's bishop one."

"Knight takes queen," Frederick said with a smile. "Check."

Maria could see the consternation in Antonio's furrowed brow, but it was only momentary. He knew it was a bluff designed to rattle his concentration, so he remained cautious.

"King takes knight," he said with a grin while gingerly removing the piece from the board. Antonio had let his guard down, and almost paid the price.

The stables were three buildings located about an acre from the back of the house. Cristo casually strolled to the entrance of the largest building which housed the riding horses. While he had finished dressing in the safety of the bathroom, Isabella had informed him that she would go ahead to the stables and get the horses ready, but before she left the room Cristo heard her try the bathroom door to see if it was locked.

Stepping into the stable, he saw Isabella in one of the stalls grooming a chestnut colored mare. She didn't hear him come in, so he took the opportunity to watch her. His eyes glanced up and down her form, admiring every curve. There was no denying that she was a beautiful young woman. If circumstances were different he would gladly give in to her, but he had made a promise to himself that he felt obligated to keep. If nothing else, he could at least indulge in the guilty pleasure of this voyeurism.

Isabella finished brushing the mare and stepped out of the stall. Instinctively, Cristo tried to slip back around the corner, but he tripped over a bucket and went sprawling on the floor. He scrambled to his feet, but not quickly enough to keep Isabella from seeing what had happened.

"My, aren't you the clumsy one," she said while trying to hold back her laughter.

"I wasn't watching where I was going," Cristo muttered while brushing the hay from his clothing.

"You poor thing, let me help you with that." Isabella walked over and began to brush away the dried grass. "I hope I wasn't the reason you were distracted."

"Oh, no. I was just looking around and. . ." But Isabella had again placed a finger against his lips.

"Please, you are not a very good liar. You don't have the experience…yet." She leaned in to kiss him, but Cristo grabbed her by the shoulders and held her back.

"No, Isabella."

She looked at him with wide eyes, then she turned and walked over to where the horses were tethered.

Cristo knew that he should let it go, but he was angry. He was used to women making passes at him, but they had always respected his wish to keep things platonic. Isabella, however, actually seemed to take offense at being turned down.

He strode over to her and asked, "Why do you feel the need to be so forward? Don't you realize that it is very unladylike and would be an embarrassment to your parents if they knew how you behaved?"

Isabella spun around, her eyes piercing. "You don't understand what it is like to be here in this place. I have no freedom. My father wasn't prepared to have a daughter. He wanted a son, someone to follow in his footsteps, to be the ladies man that both he and your father were in their youth. Instead he got me, and the thought of me meeting someone like him frightens him terribly."

Cristo was stunned. He could see the tears building in the young woman's eyes, but he had no idea of what to do. "I didn't realize..."

"Of course you didn't. No one ever thinks about what I go through. That is why I attend an all-girl's boarding school. Here I am, eighteen years old and ready for the convent, which is what my father surely wants. My mother has convinced him that was a bit drastic, so instead they decided that they would pick the man I'm to marry. That way, they will have kept me nice and pure and delivered me to the man of their choosing."

"Isabella, I understand how you feel. Even I..."

"Please, don't say anything. Just leave me alone." She turned and began to cry.

Cristo stood for a moment, then hung his head and walked back toward the house. He stopped by the pool, took off his shoes and socks, then sat on the edge with his feet dangling in the water. The water was cool, but he barely felt it.

He gazed into the distance and sighed. He had no experience with this sort of thing. Women were a mystery to him, and the things that Isabella had just said caught him off guard. It was ironic that neither one of them were the type of children their parents had expected, and to a certain degree, they both were disappointments.

The room was deathly quiet. The play was becoming intense, and Frederick and Antonio were deep in thought. Maria could see tiny beads of perspiration on the brows of both men; the battle of will and strategy taking its toll.

"Pawn takes pawn," Antonio spoke.

Frederick reached out to the board, paused, then made his move. "Bishop to king's knight seven."

"Rook to queen's rook six," Antonio replied.

"Rook takes rook."

The silence grew heavier as Antonio thought out his next move. The match had reached a point where every moved had to be carefully examined, counter-moves played out in their entirety. They were both looking for the slightest mistake to exploit.

Finally satisfied, Antonio moved. "Rook to king's knight one."

"Pawn to Queen's rook five," Frederick countered. Maria saw what was about to happen a split second before her husband released the pawn, but there was nothing she could do.

"Rook takes bishop. Check." A small smile curled on Antonio's lips. It was his first check of the match, and his host was not pleased.

Frederick had thought the match was progressing like he planned, but obviously he had made a mistake and allowed his friend to capitalize. Now, with his concentration thrown, he could feel his emotions coming to the surface.

He took a deep breath, then slowly let it out. In as calm a voice as he could muster, he turned to Maria and asked, "My dear, would you mind getting my cigarettes for me? I believe I left them on the patio table."

Maria nodded and hurried out of the room. She could see that her husband was rattled by the check and needed a moment to regain his composure. And for the first time that day, the children were the furthest thing from her mind.

Isabella closed the stable door and began walking back toward the house. Her eyes were puffy and bloodshot and her face streaked from tears, but she had managed to compose herself before walking back towards the house.

She didn't know why she had gotten so angry at Cristo, why she had lashed out at him. She felt bad for sending him away, but the way he held her off was infuriating. Men were usually falling over themselves to impress her, to try and seduce her, but Cristo didn't do anything. She could tell he was interested, it was in his eyes, the way they flickered up and down her body. For some reason he was able to hold himself in check. The worst part was that the whole thing was making her want him even more. At first it had just been for fun, but now it was becoming a quest.

As she neared the house she saw Cristo sitting on the edge of the pool. She hesitated for a moment, then walked over and joined him. He seemed surprised when she sat down beside him, and for a few minutes neither of them spoke.

Finally, Isabella said, "I'm sorry I lost my temper with you."

Cristo looked up. "Don't apologize. I guess I asked for it. I should be the one apologizing to you. I didn't mean to upset you like that..."

Isabella interrupted him, "It's over and done with. I know what your intentions are." She reached out to touch his cheek and Cristo made as if to pull away, but didn't. Isabella saw his gaze soften, then slowly, he leaned in toward her. Their lips met, barely touching, then it was over.

Isabella smiled and said, "But you still deserve this."

Realization dawned on Cristo a moment too late. Isabella gave him a solid push, and he went sideways into the pool. Her laughter was cut off seconds later when Cristo surfaced, grabbed her by the legs, and pulled her into the cold water.

They came to the surface and wiped the water from their eyes, both laughing, then swam to the side. Isabella moved closer to Cristo, brushing his hair back from his face, and this time he didn't flinch. With one hand on the edge of the pool, he wrapped his other arm around her waist and pulled her body tight against his.

This time the kiss was not as gentle.

The house was quiet as Maria walked through to the patio and she wondered where Isabella and Cristo were, but the thought quickly passed as she stepped through the French doors and into the fresh air. The sun was beginning to sink into the afternoon sky, casting the first shadows across the yard.

She was just reaching for the pack of cigarettes on the table when a movement in the pool caught her attention. It took a moment for the image to sink in.

"Isabella! What in God's name are you doing?"

Both Isabella and Cristo froze as Maria came striding around the pool, her face flushed and eyes wide.

"Have you lost your mind? What would your father say if he were to find out about this? Get out of that pool this instant. No daughter of mine will act like a woman of loose morals. My God, you have embarrassed this family! Go, to your room, and do not show your face to me until I say so."

Isabella climbed out of the pool and ran to the house, covering her face. Maria then turned to Cristo, who had climbed out as well. "I expect better behavior from guests in my house. Out of respect for your father, I will not mention this incident to him, but I do not think you will be welcome in my house again for a very long time."

Cristo opened his mouth to speak, but before he could say a word Maria turned and went back into the house.

Maria was still trembling and red-faced when she returned with her husband's cigarettes, but the two friends were too involved with their chess match to notice.

Frederick lit a cigarette, then exhaled a plume of gray smoke and sighed. "Ahh, that is better. Now, where were we?"

"I believe it is your move, mi amigo," Antonio replied.

"Very well, then. King to king three."

"Rook to king's bishop two."

"Pawn to king six. Check," Frederick said as his smile returned.

"King takes pawn," Antonio announced.

Frederick's grin grew wider.

Isabella sat up in bed when she heard the soft knock at her door. She closed her robe and crossed the room to see who it was, expecting her mother. Instead, she was surprised to see Cristo standing in the hallway.

"I came to apologize, again."

"What for? You did nothing wrong. I instigated it, only this time my mother saved you," Isabella replied with a hint of disappointment. "I'm sorry she embarrassed you like that."

"Oh, no, she didn't. Really. I just wanted to come and make sure that you..."

"Would you like to come in and keep me company for a while?"

"I guess so," Cristo said quickly.

Isabella stood back and let him in, then softly closed the door and turned the lock.

Antonio could not believe his predicament. None of his strategies had worked; his defenses had been useless and his offensive moves seemingly ineffective. Now he was backed into a corner with nothing left to do but prolong the inevitable.

"Queen takes pawn. Check," Frederick spoke.

"King to King's bishop four." Antonio knew what was coming, but he felt like a rabbit frozen in fear as the hawk swooped down upon him. He was being swept along in a game in which he had no control.

"I guess we got off on the wrong foot today," Isabella said. Cristo sat on the edge of her bed while she lay propped up against the pillows.

"I agree," Cristo replied without looking at her.

"I hope you were able to change out of those wet clothes before you caught a cold."

Cristo grinned and said, "Yes, and I bet you wish you could have been there to help."

She smiled and slid down the bed to sit closer to him. Cristo knew what was coming as she moved her body against his. As he turned to look at her, their lips met, and he felt his inhibitions slip away.

Maria knew that Frederick was on the verge of taking the match, but she couldn't stop fidgeting in her chair. If her husband felt any apprehension, it did not show on his face. He had been beaten too many times by his friend not to savor this victory. He could see the resignation in Antonio's eyes. His time was drawing to a close.

"Queen takes pawn. Check." He could almost see Antonio winch at the words.

Across the table, Antonio stroked his chin for a moment, then responded. "King to king's bishop three."

Frederick looked at his wife and winked. Time for the final move.

Cristo and Isabella fell back onto the bed, bodies entwined as they rolled across the mattress. Cristo felt his heart pounding in his chest and the blood roaring in his ears. He had never experienced such intensity of emotion. Every nerve ending was alive as they tumbled back and forth, hands exploring and caressing. They stopped with Isabella on top, her robe barely held closed by the sash.

"I don't think I can do this," Cristo panted, grasping her by the shoulders.

"Don't think," was her reply. She sat up and untied her robe, letting it fall from her shoulders.

Cristo smiled and pulled her back down on top of him.

"Any last requests?" Frederick asked.

"Yes, I would like one of those cigarettes," Antonio replied.

Frederick slid the pack across the table and waited for his friend to light one.

"I have been waiting for this day for quite a while," Frederick said, "queen to king-five. Check mate."

The sun was setting behind the mountains when Antonio and his son decided to take a walk through the garden. Maria was in the kitchen trying to make dinner as Fredrick replayed the match for her in excessive detail.

After their encounter earlier, Isabella had softly kissed Cristo then left the room. Cristo had expected to feel used, but instead he found that he was relieved, as if a burden had been lifted. He continued to lay in her bed for a while, enjoying the scent of her perfume on the sheets and the breeze blowing through the open window. He finally rose, reluctantly, and went downstairs.

As father and son came to the edge of the garden, they saw Isabella galloping across a distant field on a beautiful roan, her dark hair billowing out behind her as she chased the wind.

"So," Antonio began, "did you enjoy your afternoon with Isabella?"

Cristo let out a slight cough as the breath caught in his throat. "It was nice. We...went for a swim."

"Good, good. I am glad to hear you enjoyed yourself. I was afraid that she might be a bit too brash for you."

"Oh, no, father. We got along quite well."

Antonio looked his son in the face for a moment, then continued walking.

"I am sorry you lost your chess match," Cristo said, trying to change the subject.

"It is nothing. I had a good run for a while there, but it had to end. My strategies are not what they used to be. Now I go back and try to prepare for the next time we play."

They walked for a few moments in silence, then Cristo asked, "Father, do you think you could teach me how to play?"

"Of course, son," he replied, "I think that you would be quite good at the game. You've had plenty of practice dodging the ladies. As I tried to explain to our host earlier, chess is like a seduction, or the avoidance of one. Your opponent tries to trick you into letting your guard down, then takes you."

"I think I understand."

"Good. That was your first lesson, to never let your guard down. That is how you end up in check-mate. But I don't think you'll have a problem with that."

Cristo smiled at his father and said, "I may not be as good as you think."

Antonio put an arm around the young man's shoulders. "Not to worry, my son. Sometimes losing has its own rewards."

'ROIDS

It isn't every day that you see someone get shot. At least, it isn't a common occurrence in my life. I was walking out of the drug store when I saw this guy walking towards me. I generally don't pay much attention to other people, especially strangers on the street, but this guy caught my attention. I think it was the look on his face, the firm line of his mouth, the dead look in his eyes, and the fact he was a massive compilation of muscle. He strode across the asphalt like a laser-guided nuclear missile. Or like one pissed off son of a bitch. One hand clutched a brown paper bag while the other was clenched into a massive fist.

He bumped my shoulder as he walked by me, hard enough to spin me around and make me drop my bag. I started to say something but the look on his face warned me otherwise. It's a good thing, too. Just as he passes me, and while I'm still spinning, he reaches into his brown bag and suddenly there's a gun in his hand. Before I could react he lifts the gun and opens fire on the guy behind me, some clerk or something who had just gotten off work. He had his work coat slung over his shoulder and an envelope in his hand.

The first bullet caught him on the outside of his left shoulder. I saw the material of his shirt rip and a hole appear in the glass door behind him. The clerk looked down at the wound as if he wasn't sure what just happened. The next shot got him square in the chest. His mouth opened into a wide "O" and he fell backwards onto the sidewalk. The shooter leaned over his fallen victim and said, "That'll teach you to fuck another man's wife." Then he turned and walked away, not even looking at me.

I stood there unsure of what to do, my recent purchase of hemorrhoid cream forgotten on the sidewalk. I watched the gunman cross the parking lot and climb into a faded blue and rust covered pick-up truck. A moment later he was pulling into traffic, leaving behind a haze of gray smoke. I turned back to the clerk laying on the ground not five feet away. I took a step towards him with the heart pounding in my chest, but one look told me there was nothing I could do. Several people came running out of the store and knelt around him. I could hear screaming and crying coming from behind the doors. I felt something on my face and wiped at it with the back of my hand. I was surprised to see that it was tears.

It was three more hours before I got home. The cops had me go over my story a dozen times, asking me why I didn't jump the shooter, why I didn't follow him to the parking lot and get his tag number, why I didn't do anything. I don't know about you, but there's no way in hell I'm screwing around with a guy carrying a gun. Hell, he'd just shot someone. And I'm supposed to intervene? I don't think so. The way I was fidgeting probably didn't help matters. But what could I do? I decided to just deal with it until they let me go. I just hadn't realized how long that would be.

Walking up the stairs to my apartment was one of the more uncomfortable experiences of my life. I almost fell on floor the after I got the door opened, and I had my pants off by the time I made it to the bathroom. I applied the hemorrhoid cream liberally then laid on the floor and waited for it to work. In the meantime I thought about the things the cops were saying to me. Was I a coward for not making an attempt to stop the guy with the gun? Was there anything I could have done to save that clerk's life? I hated second guessing myself. I had enough of that with Margie both before and after she left me. That woman had me so screwed up I didn't know what the hell I was doing. She was the reason I started having hemorrhoid problems. The divorce proceedings were making it worse.

The last letter I received from her attorney informed me that she wanted me to pay twenty-five hundred dollars a month in alimony. Her argument is that she has a bad back and can't work, so I should make sure she is supported until such a time that she can return to work. In other words, she wants an early retirement. The alimony will pay the mortgage on her double-wide trailer and the lien on her new truck with a little left over for alcohol.

The cream finally started working, so I pulled up my pants, washed my hands, then went into the kitchen to heat up a microwave dinner. Nothing like home cooking, I told myself. Except for the microwave and the refrigerator, the kitchen was spotless. I hadn't used the stove or oven since I moved in three months ago, and microwave dinners eaten with plastic utensils cut down on the wear and tear of the sink area. I'm all for efficiency. Besides, I never learned to cook and I hated doing dishes.

I plopped down on the couch with my dinner resting on my lap and turned on the television. The local news was doing a report on the shooting. The reporter's face took up most of the screen, but just over her shoulder I could see myself being interviewed by the cops. I was in profile and I think I looked pretty good considering what I had just been through.

I almost spit out my meatloaf when they cut to a close-up of me giving my statement, a graphic under my chin stating that I was the only witness. And with that they included my name. I put my tray down on the coffee table and sat back on the couch. My stomach felt funny, all knotted up and gurgling. I wasn't good at dealing with shit like this. Here I was, the only witness to a murder and they're flashing my mug on the evening news. I ran my hands through my hair and cussed, then I got up and headed back to the bathroom. My ass was itching again.

There was hell to pay the next morning when I got to work. An endless succession of coworkers felt the need to stop by my cubicle to let me know they had seen me on the news and ask me what had happened. At first I wasn't sure what to say. Well, that's not exactly true. I had a few ideas, but none of them were very polite. I kept repeating that I really didn't know, only that the guy had been shot by a jealous husband or something and I didn't want to talk about it. By afternoon the procession had ended, only to be replaced with furtive glances and whispers about "witness trauma". At least the hemorrhoid cream was working and I was able to sit still for eight hours on my doughnut pillow while punching sales figures in the database.

At four fifty-five I was ready to get home. I turned off my computer, grabbed my coat and hurried to the door. Unfortunately, I was in such a rush to get out of there that I didn't notice the news crew standing in the parking lot. I heard a woman's voice call my name, then the next thing I knew there was a camera lens and microphone in my face.

"Mr. Humbert," the young female reporter said as she blocked the path to my car. "Marcia Marconi, Live at Five News. How do you feel knowing that Tommy Miller's killer is still on the loose?"

"I hadn't really thought about it." I tried to walk around her, but she sidestepped and blocked my escape.

"But aren't you worried that he might come after you next?"

I could see where this was going. She wanted to play hardball, and that was fine by me. Being married to Margie was like going through verbal-sparring boot camp. I'd been trained by the best of them.

"Well, I wasn't until you mentioned it. I sure hope he doesn't watch your program."

That one froze her in her tracks. Even her videographer stopped filming and took a look at me from behind the camera. I took the opportunity to finish the walk to my car. I had the engine started before Marcia and her cameraman caught up with me, but it was too late for them to keep me from making my getaway. The tires squealed as I pulled out of the parking lot, merely by accident, but I'm sure it must have seemed like I was high-tailing it out of there. Truth be told, it made me feel like a badass.

The encounter with the reporter had got my hemorrhoids stirring. I had my ointment in the tote bag sitting on the seat next to me, but I didn't think it would be feasible to try to apply it while commuting through rush hour traffic. I just stayed focused on getting home as quickly as possible while trying to ignore the intense itching coming from my nether regions.

I guess there's such a thing as being too focused. I wasn't paying attention to my speed as I neared my apartment complex, and I sure as hell didn't see the motorcycle cop parked on a side street with a radar gun. I was about a hundred yards from my front door when he pulled me over. By the time he walked up to me I had already pulled out my license and insurance card, hoping to make the ticket writing process as quick as possible, but I had a hard time sitting still, which, of course, caught the cop's attention.

"Got a problem there, buddy?" he asked without bothering to stop writing the ticket.

"Medical condition, officer," I replied.

"Ants in your pants?"

I figured it was some sort of cop joke. I wasn't in the mood to laugh.

"No, actually I have a bad case of hemorrhoids. I was hurrying to get home so I could apply some medicine."

"That so?" he asked. "Maybe I should run your license, just to make sure."

I leaned back into the headrest and closed my eyes. The itching was reaching that point where it becomes unbearable, but what could I do? I glanced in the mirror and saw the cop standing behind my car speaking into his shoulder radio. After what seemed liked hours, he walked back up and handed me my license and the speeding ticket.

"So you're the guy who witnessed that murder yesterday. You know we still haven't caught the killer yet, so you'd better be careful."

With that he turned and walked back to his motorcycle. I didn't waste any time in getting my car started and driving the rest of the way home.

I could hear the phone ringing as I unlocked the door, but I wasn't quick enough to grab it before the answering machine picked up.

"Mr. Humbert? This is Connie O'Steen at the Journal-Sentinel. I was hoping to talk to you about the murder you witnessed and get your comments on the aftereffects you've had to deal with. You can reach me at..."

I reached down to hit the "erase" button when I noticed the message light flashing with the number of calls I had received. One-hundred and twenty. In one day. I hit the playback and listened from the bathroom as I applied a soothing dose of ointment to my overheated ass.

Although the voices were different, the messages were almost all alike. Each one was a reporter from some news outlet asking me to call them back for an interview, or a comment, or for my opinion. Then the same reporters calling back to let me know they were on deadline. I washed my hands and turned off the machine just as the phone began to ring. I lifted the receiver then hung it right back up. After a count of three I took the handset out of the cradle and laid it on the counter. I wasn't up for dealing with anymore phone calls tonight. I needed to get some dinner and relax.

Three minutes and forty-five seconds later (which is how long it takes for my Mama Mia Frozen Entrée to heat up), the doorbell rang. I took a step towards the door, then hesitated. I wasn't expecting anyone to come over, and the few friends I retained after the divorce weren't the type to just pop over without notice. I crept to the door and looked out the peephole. A reporter and a cameraman were standing on the other side. I'd seen the reporter on one of the local news stations, young and full of ego. He liked to ask probing questions of the victims of tragedy, stuff like, "So your husband was run over by a bus. How does that make you feel?"

I sure as hell wasn't going to subject myself to his cutting edge news reporting. I walked back to the kitchen to retrieve my dinner, then settled down on my doughnut pillow to watch some television. The reporter rang the bell three more times, then proceeded to knock for almost ten minutes. I figured he and his cameraman must have been waiting in the parking lot for me to get home so they could corner me in my own doorway. He probably had me pegged for one of those schleps who can't wait to get in front of a camera and ramble on like some babbling idiot. People like that annoy me. I just want to be left alone. Besides, the cops still hadn't caught the gunman. All I needed to do was get on television and say something stupid to have the guy come after me.

The reporter finally got tired of knocking, or maybe he bruised his knuckles, but for the rest of the evening the front door was silent. Before I went to bed I turned off all the lights in the apartment and peeked out through the blinds. Down in the parking lot I could see three news vans, and across the street was another. They were like predators waiting in the dark for me to let my guard down. Before I headed to the bedroom I stopped and made a quick phone call. I was on to their tricks, and I wasn't going to let the bastards catch me.

The next morning the news trucks were still there. I finished getting dressed and watched them from my front window as I sipped my coffee. Fast food wrappers littered the dashboards and I could only imagine what it must have smelled like inside after they spent the night in there. I hoped they were uncomfortable. Satisfied with a final happy thought, I went to the back of the apartment and glanced out my bedroom window. The rear parking lot was mostly empty, just a couple of cars and a pickup truck. I waited a couple of minutes, then sighed with relief when I saw Joe pull into the parking lot. He was one of the few people at work that I could tolerate for short periods of time. He rolled his car into an empty space and tooted the horn.

Feeling energized by the fact that my plan to evade the reporters was working, I checked my pockets to make sure I had my wallet, keys, and ointment, then I opened the window and climbed out onto the small ledge below it. To my right was an iron ladder bolted to the side of the building. The maintenance crews used it to get to the roof for repairs. I shimmied over to it, then climbed down. Joe was watching from the front seat of his car, his mouth hanging open as I strode across the sidewalk and into the parking lot.

It was then that I heard another engine revving, and suddenly there was a blue pickup truck screeching to a halt between me and Joe's car. My first instinct was that a reporter had gotten smart and caught me, but when I saw the barrel of the .45 sticking out the driver's side window I knew I was in trouble.

"Get in."

It was him, the gunman from the day before. He'd found me. I licked my lips and quickly looked around for help. Joe was still sitting in his car on the other side of the truck so he couldn't see what was going on, and as far as I could tell there was no one else about.

"I'm not going to tell you again, get in the fucking truck," the gunman yelled.

I walked around the front of the truck and was relieved to make eye contact with Joe before I climbed into the cab. As I reached for the door handle with my right hand, I made a finger gun with my left and made a motion as if I was pulling the trigger. Joe merely looked puzzled and began to roll down his window, but before either one of us could say anything I climbed into the truck. The gunman hit the gas and we tore out of the parking lot with a squeal of tires.

"So, you're the guy I bumped into yesterday?" the driver asked. His scarred knuckles were white with strain as he gripped the worn steering wheel.

"Uh, yeah," I replied while keeping one hand on the door handle and looking for a place to jump out.

"Hang on," he said as he whipped around a corner. "Oh, and that door won't open from the inside. Handle's broke."

"Duly noted," I signed. "So, um, where are we going?"

"Nowhere in particular," he said.

"Okay." I had no idea what to do, but I figured I needed to ask the big question. "So, why did you just kidnap me?"

"Oh, this ain't no kidnapping," the driver laughed. "I just wanted to talk to you."

"At gunpoint," I added.

"Well, I needed you to get in the truck. Couldn't just walk up to your front door and knock, not with all them news folk out there."

"But how did you know I'd climb out my back window?"

"I didn't. Just luck. I'd been parked out there a while tryin' to figure out how to get in touch with you. Then you just showed up. Crazy, ain't it?" He looked at me and winked.

"Yep, that's the word," I said.

We pulled up to a stop light and the truck wheezed to a slow halt. The driver stuck a beefy hand in my direction and said, "Name's Wayne."

I looked at his calloused hand and wondered what I was supposed to do. On a whim, I shook.

"Henry," I offered.

"Please to meet'cha," Wayne said with a smile. He squirmed a little in his seat, then punched the gas when the light turned green.

"So, Wayne, what's next?"

"Well, here's the thing," he pointed to a six-pack cooler on the floor near my feet. "Can you hand me a beer?"

I pulled a lukewarm can from the cooler, popped the top, and handed it to him.

"See," he continued, "I sort of lost my temper the other day. Found out my old lady was messin' around with the assistant pharmacist there at Drug-Co and about lost my damn mind."

"I see," I replied, even though I didn't. "I assume your wife knows what you did?"

Wayne fidgeted a bit at my question, then took a long pull off his can of beer.

"Actually, she doesn't. She's dead, too."

I could feel my ass start to itch and wondered if Wayne would pull over so I could apply some ointment. I just wasn't sure where this conversation was heading and didn't want to provoke an obviously unstable individual.

Wayne finished off his beer and tossed the empty can out his window. "See, I'm not a violent man. I just been havin' some issues lately…"

"Issues, right…," I said. I had my hand back on the door handle and was slowing working it back and forth. It was loose, but for a moment I felt it catch on something.

"It's health related, you know. Personal stuff. A man can't really talk about some of that stuff."

"Sure, man stuff." The door handle caught again. This time it held. I got ready to yank it hard and jump.

"And it gets me all aggravated. Short temper...when I found the love notes in her make up table...you know what I'm sayin'?"

"Make up table..." I mumbled. Time to go. I yanked on the door handle and felt the latch pop. The door was just about to swing open when I heard Wayne cuss.

"Shit. Cops up there. Hold on."

He whipped the truck to the right. The passenger door that had just started to open closed back with a pop and the door handle came off in my hand. Now my hemorrhoids were really angry. I squirmed in my seat to find a comfortable position as Wayne forced his clunker to pick up speed. He wove his way through the backstreets like a NASCAR driver on meth.

"See, the thing is," he continued. "I was havin' a bad day with my...health issues when I found out Lisa was cheatin' on me. I just lost it."

"Right," I replied through gritted teeth. "And you're telling me this because?"

"I just needed someone to talk to, you know? Hand me another beer, willya'?"

I popped the top on another can and handed it to him as he adjusted his position behind the wheel.

"But why me?" I asked.

"Why not? You were there, man. You saw what happened."

"Right," I replied. "And?"

"And? Hell, we're like kindred spirits."

"Um, my wife is still alive," I said. Not that I was happy about it.

"Oh, for some reason I thought you were livin' alone."

"I am," I said. "But we're getting divorced."

Wayne thumped the dashboard with his hand and the whole truck shook. "Don't you see? Kindred spirits, man."

"I still don't see..."

"And you probably have some health issues, too, right?" He looked at me with wide eyes and a grin that showed his yellowed teeth.

"Um, well, yeah," I replied as I squirmed in my seat. The busted springs were less than comfortable.

Wayne maneuvered the truck towards the city limits. I didn't like where we were heading. The woods on this side of town were thick and sparsely populated. I was still working on the door handle to see if I could get it to catch again.

"Me, it's them damn 'roids, man," Wayne said in a low voice. He was leaning close to the steering wheel with his eyes focused on the road ahead.

That confession got my attention. "'Roids? As in hemorrhoids?"

Wayne looked at me and barked a laugh. "Nah, man, that's fucked up. No, I mean steroids, you know? Body building stuff. You don't think I got this big just painting houses, do you?"

I felt a wave of disappointment wash over me. For whatever reason, I thought that having a connection would somehow work in my favor.

"My old lady kept telling me to bulk up," Wayne continued. "So I figured I'd get 'roided up. Bulk up real fast, you know? Didn't realize it would mess me up like it did. I mean, I got the muscles she was wanting, but, well, other stuff stopped working right."

It took me a moment to realize what he was referring to.

"Um, couldn't you just stop taking the steroids and that would start working again?"

"That's what I thought, my man, but the doctor said I took too much."

He turned the truck down a dirt road that wove between the pine trees. The branches were like a canopy over the road, blocking most of the sunlight and dropping the temperature a noticeable degree. The bumpiness of the road and the damn broken springs were making my life hell, but I kept my discomfort to myself as best I could.

"That's, well, that's too bad," I said as I wondered how much longer I had to live. "But you never know, maybe things will get better."

We ended up in a clearing near a pond. Wayne put the truck in park and the engine protested for another minute or so after he turned the key. He finished his current beer and I handed him another one before he asked. I figured that making myself useful might buy me some time.

"So, um, nice place," I said as I looked out through the dirty windshield.

"Yeah, it is. Used to fish that pond when I was a kid."

I nodded and fidgeted in my seat. I needed relief.

"Listen," I said, trying to keep my voice as calm as possible. "I need to step behind a tree for a moment…"

Wayne looked at me and nodded. "That's fine. Hang on while I open that door for you."

He got out and walked around the truck. He yanked the door and it opened with the sound of metal on metal. I patted my coat pocket to make sure the ointment was still there, then hurried behind a tree and dropped my pants. Relief wasn't instant, but I knew it was on the way. Once I finished the application I wiped my fingers on the tree trunk and got them covered in pine sap. Wonderful. I walked back to the truck trying to wipe my sticky fingers on my pant leg.

"Figured you'd try to run off," Wayne said from the cab of the truck.

"Where would I go? I have no idea where we are?"

He nodded and took another pull off his beer. "So you and your old lady are divorcing? You leave her or she leave you?"

I sighed, stuck my hands in my pockets, then looked over at the pond. "She left. Well, she kicked me out of the house we were renting."

"Whaddya do?"

"I guess I just wasn't doing it for her. I don't know." I shook my head and looked at the humongous man sitting in the truck. "She never actually said. The divorce papers say 'irreconcilable differences', which I think is legalese for 'no longer in love'."

"So you two just drifted apart? I guess that's better than cheatin'."

"No, I wouldn't say we drifted apart. Really, I'm not sure if we were ever in love. It was just one of those things. We dated for a while, seemed to get along, got married. It was her idea. But then, she never got a job or anything. I worked, she stayed home and, well, she just got meaner and meaner."

"And you didn't do anything to provoke her?" Wayne asked, his eyebrows narrowed.

"No, not a thing. I tried to make her happy. I bought her things, bigger television, new computer, got her a car. None of it was good enough."

Wayne shook his head. "Damn, son, it sounds like she thought you were her meal ticket. Now what?"

I walked around to the passenger side of the truck and climbed into the cab. "I don't know. She's basically taken me for everything, plus a couple of grand a month for support. I'm broke. Completely. And I'll probably need to get another job to make ends meet."

Wayne was silent for a few minutes, then suddenly he slammed his almost empty beer can on the dashboard. Warm beer splashed against the inside of the windshield and on both of us.

"Damn, that shit pisses me off!" His face was beet red and his eyes were bulging. "A decent guy like you getting' screwed over by some woman for no reason."

He slid out of the truck and began pacing back and forth in the tall grass. He was mumbling to himself and gesturing as if he was arguing with someone.

"You okay?" I called out.

I watched him pause and take a deep breath. That seemed to help. The color in his face went from beet red to just red. He climbed back into the truck and looked at me. I could see his nostrils flaring.

"I'm screwed, ain't I?" he asked.

"I'm not sure what…"

"The murders. You know, I killed my old lady and the pharmacy guy, right? So I'm screwed."

I shrugged. "I guess so. I mean, I don't know all the details of your situation, but two murders is kinda bad and…"

"Right. So I might as well try and do something good, right?"

Again, I shrugged. "I don't think you can just…"

"You're right," he said and punched me in the shoulder. It felt as if I'd been hit with a brick, but I managed to keep from yelling out in pain.

Wayne started the engine. There was a loud backfire and we were soon engulfed in blue exhaust. He put the truck in gear and spun us around. In a few minutes we were heading down the dirt road.

Wayne didn't speak again until we hit the paved road. By now the ointment had taken the edge off the itchiness, but the ride was far from comfortable. When we got to the main road he slammed on the brakes and the truck rolled to a stop.

"Where are we going now?" I asked.

"You tell me," Wayne replied.

"I don't understand."

"Where's your ex live?"

I felt something tighten in my chest. "I don't think…"

"I'm going to fix this for you!" he yelled as he rocked back and forth behind the wheel. The truck weaved back and forth between the white lines for a few hundred feet.

"Okay, okay," I said, my hand gripping the dashboard.

Wayne took a deep breath. "Sorry 'bout that. Temper gets away from me sometimes. Now, where does your ex live?"

I told him the name of the road.

"Oh, yeah, that ain't too far from here."

He took a few turns at unsafe speed, and within a few minutes we were pulling onto the shoulder of the road about a quarter of a mile from the brand new double-wide trailer. I could see the brand new F-150 parked in the driveway.

"That the place?" Wayne asked.

I nodded. "Yeah, she bought it after she cleaned out our savings account."

"What's her name?"

"Beatrice," I replied. "Listen, I don't think you should go knock on the door and confront her about…"

"Nope, not what I'm gonna do. I assume that's her truck parked out front? Wanna hand me another beer?"

I nodded and pulled the last one out of the cooler, popped the top, and handed it to him. He drained half the can and leaned back in his seat.

"Why dontcha get out here. You don't need to be seen."

"What are you going to do?"

"Don't you worry about that." He stepped out of the truck and walked around to my side to open the door. "In fact, you should probably start walking back to your place."

"That's several miles," I replied as I looked up and down the empty road. "No taxis out this way, are there?"

Wayne laughed and smacked me on the back. I couldn't breathe for a moment and coughed for a good two minutes. I figured that was going to leave a ham-sized bruise between my shoulder blades.

"Naw, man. But there's a convenience store back past the intersection. You can get there in about five minutes on foot, I'm sure. Now git."

He gave me a gentle shove and I started walking down the side of the road, my legs swishing through the tall grass and wildflowers. I was considering looking back, but just as I thought I shouldn't I heard the truck engine rev up. I turned and heard Wayne slip the transmission into gear with a clank. The back tires spun in the dirt, then found purchase on the road and began accelerating.

I expected him to slow down when he made it to the driveway, but instead he cut the wheel and slid into the dirt driveway. The truck was blowing gray smoke across the front yard and I thought I heard Wayne laugh just before the truck plowed through the propane tank and into the trailer. There was an explosion, which was probably the propane, then a second explosion, which I attributed to the gas tank on the truck. Between the two, the trailer went up in a million little pieces. I saw the fireball rise in slow motion, then I saw the shockwave flow across the tall grass like a green wave. I was far enough away that it just felt like a warm breeze when it reached me. The sound of the explosions were just a moment behind.

I was still standing there twenty minutes later when the fire truck and two sheriff's deputies came up the road with sirens wailing. While the firemen did their job, one of the deputies noticed me and drove over. He ended up giving me a ride home.

With Beatrice's death, I was off the hook for any alimony payments. Oddly enough, she hadn't yet taken me off her life insurance yet. I'm sure that was an oversight. The payout was enough to get me out of debt and helped me buy a nice little house in a quiet part of town. I was questioned by the investigators a couple of times, but the story was cut and dry. I was kidnapped by the guy who murdered his wife and the man she was having an affair with, a kidnapping witnessed by my coworker. A few hours later he kicked me out of his truck and drove into my exes house. I was honest with my answers to the questions. I don't know why he did it or why he kidnapped me. I assumed they would find steroids in his system during the autopsy.

But that's the weird thing here. They didn't find his body. They found Beatrice partially incinerated, but there was still enough of her left for identification. Wayne, however, was gone. The conclusion was that he was burned up in the blaze.

Personally, I'm not so sure. He was one big son of a bitch and that was a lot to burn up into nothing. Every now and then when I see some random road rage incident reported on the local news I wonder if it's him.

LAST RITES

The last time I saw my brother was at our father's funeral.

It was an August afternoon. I stepped out of my car and immediately felt my white dress shirt stick to my torso. I reached into the back seat and grabbed my suit coat, slipping it on as beads of sweat began to form on my forehead. North Florida in summer is unforgiving. It reminded me of the old man.

As I wove my way through the dozen or so cars in the parking lot I worried my shoes might sink into the black pavement. I could use that for an excuse to miss the festivities. But no, I made it to the front of the funeral home just fine and was greeted by the first of the mourners. An old man held out his hand as a half smile shifted the wrinkles on his face.

"Sorry about your father," he said in a low voice. "My condolences."

I shook his hand — firm grip and three pumps — and nodded in acknowledgement. As he stepped away I sighed. I would have to go through this routine a few more times before the service started. I wondered if I should have brought some hand sanitizer. That would have annoyed the hell out of my old man. He didn't worry about germs. Hell, he didn't worry about much of anything.

A small group were huddled at the front door. I knew I'd have to run the gauntlet and took a moment to prepare myself. I looked off to the East and the well-manicured cemetery that stretched across several acres of treeless greenery. Headstones of all shapes and sizes seemed to disrupt what would have otherwise been a perfect tableau. Nothing like a military cemetery, with its perfect white stones laid out in symmetrical rows. No, this was for the civvies, as the old man would say.

I was surprised he was being buried here instead of next to my mother. She had the full military send off, folded flag, and twenty-one gun salute. It was nice. She deserved it. I barely remembered it. I was only five when she died.

But then, the old man carried a chip on his shoulder. He acted military, but never made it in. Medical condition he wouldn't talk about. He met mom while bartending at a USO show, they hit it off, he ended up getting her pregnant. I doubt the marriage would have lasted much longer after I came along. While I don't have many memories of her, I do remember the loud voices late at night, the slurred insults, and waking up the next morning to find the old man sleeping it off on the couch. I had to eat my cereal while sitting close to the television with the volume down low.

I turned and flapped the edges of my coat to try and ventilate some of the moisture that was now running in streams down my torso. The shirt was too wet to soak up any more sweat. I figured I might as well head inside and see if I could catch pneumonia.

The group at the door all stopped talking as I approached. They turned to me with faces of stone and empty eyes, the men extending their hands, the women coming in close for floral-scented hugs and pecks on the cheek. There wasn't any conversation, just the same platitudes. There wasn't a teary eye to be seen. They all knew my old man. They were here because it was what they were supposed to do, to see and be seen. I barely recognized any of them. I'd been away for a long time, started a new life, tried to forget the old one. Looking into those faces I felt like I had almost succeeded.

As I reached for the door handle, one of the men put a hand on my shoulder and gave it a squeeze. "Your brother is already inside," he said.

The second-to-last time I saw my brother was ten years before that. It was at our father's retirement party. Well, more of a gathering. Parties are events with smiles and laughter, people mingling, talking, meeting and greeting. This was more like a wake. There was no music, just small groups of people standing around, shuffling their feet, not making eye contact with anyone else. At least there was alcohol. If my father was involved, there was always alcohol.

My wife had stayed home. She was six-months pregnant and going through a rough patch. I offered to stay with her, but she insisted I go. It might be good for me and my old man, spend some time together, show some support for his retirement. She had good intentions.

The old man was well into a bottle of Scotch by the time I arrived. He leaned against a folding table in the corner that served as the make-shift bar. About two dozen bottles of liquor, a bucket of ice, two short stacks of clear plastic cups. Because someone had rented a room at the local YMCA for this event, I could hear the sounds of kids playing basketball through the far wall.

My brother stood with him, weaving side to side as he finished what was left in his cup. They didn't see me arrive and I stood there by the door for a few moments preparing myself. I took a few deep breaths as the other people in the room began to notice me. That seemed to spark some quiet conversation among those who knew the family. But no one came over to say hello. They just stood and watched. Probably the best thing they could have done.

As I walked across the room, the few people who stood near the bar moved away. It was as if they could sense the impending explosion and were trying to get out of range of the shrapnel.

My old man saw me as I came near and crossed his arms, careful not to spill the watered-down Scotch he was holding in his left hand.

"About time you showed up," he said.

"Good to see you, too," I replied. "Tanya sends her regards."

"What? She too lazy to come?" my brother asked.

A referee's whistle blew on the other side of the wall.

"So, did they give you a gold watch or something?" I asked my old man.

"Nah, cheap bastards. Gave me a card and a gift certificate to a doughnut place up the street. Thirty fucking years and I get a coupon."

"Sorry to hear..."

"So your old lady don't like us or something?" my brother interjected.

I turned and looked into his bloodshot eyes. "She's not feeling well. Having some difficulties with the pregnancy."

He flashed a feral grin and stepped around the old man to pour himself another drink. "Getting too fat to get around. Too bad.

Must be hell for you to have to deal with that."

I shuffled my feet and let my breath out nice and slow. "So, pops, what are you going to do now?"

He finished his drink, then elbowed my brother and handed him the empty cup for a refill. "Don't know. Hadn't thought about it."

"Well, you could go fishing. Maybe buy a little boat and..."

"So how fat is she now?" my brother asked as he turned to face me.

My hands clenched into fists, so I stuffed them in my pockets. "Like I was saying, you could..."

"Don't ignore your brother," the old man snapped.

"I'm trying to keep this civil."

"Bullshit," the old man replied. "He's your older brother. You show him some respect."

"He needs to show me some, first."

If the room was quiet before, now it was like a dead zone. I could feel every eye in the room staring at our little tableau. Even the game on the other side of the wall had stopped.

"I'm not here for a fight. I just came to pay my respects and wish you well."

"I'm not here for a fight," my brother repeated in a falsetto. Both he and the old man laughed at that.

I wanted to lash out, to do something with the fists that were clenched in my pockets. I could feel my fingernails digging into my palms, feel my face flushing as my blood pressure rose, but instead I turned and walked out of the room. In the hallway I stopped and leaned against the concrete wall. Opposite me, a poster of a man and boy was taped to the chipped and peeling paint. They looked like they were having fun, the man teaching the boy how to swim. I felt like I was drowning.

When I stepped into the funeral home I was immediately hit with a wave of frigid air and a floral smell must have been pumped in with the air conditioning. There were a few more people inside, but the room was barely half full. There was hushed conversation and organ music was being piped in through speakers recessed in the ceiling. A shiver ran through me as the cold hit my soaked shirt. I wondered how long I could remain in here before I would get sick.

I took a few tentative steps up the center aisle, then paused, resting my hand on the back of a black metal folding chair. The room was long and narrow, with tall, frosted-glass windows on opposite walls. The casket, dark brown wood that was polished to a high gloss, lay at the other end of the aisle. The lid was open for viewing and I was torn between wanting to see the old man one last time and not wanting to see him dead. Not that I had many fond memories of him, but I wasn't sure I wanted this to be my last memory of him.

But my legs began to move and I found myself standing next to the coffin. The old man was dressed in a dark blue suit and smelled of Old Spice. Even in death his facial expression hadn't changed: Furrowed brow, corners of his mouth turned down, eyes closed but the lids were scrunched up. He was carrying that chip on his shoulder into the afterlife.

I tried to think of something positive about him, but was interrupted by hearing my name mentioned. I looked over my shoulder to see my brother sitting in the front row speaking to a veiled old woman. I almost didn't recognize him. His hair had thinned out and what was left of it was a dirty gray color. Dark lines creased his face and his nose was lit up with busted blood vessels. For a moment I thought it was the ghost of the old man come to watch his own send off.

He glanced over and we made eye contact, but I wasn't in the mood for a confrontation, so I turned away and walked to the back of the room to sit down. The chair was stiff and uncomfortable. When I leaned back the cold metal pressed into my still-wet shirt and made every muscle in my body clench up. I took a deep breath of perfumed air and waited.

Prior to my father's retirement party, I hadn't seen my brother in about five years. I had invited him to my wedding, but he didn't show for the ceremony. At least, that's what I was told. I was too busy being nervous and excited to care one way or another. But a friend of mine who knew the situation kept an eye out for him, ready to step in if need be to prevent him from ruining the day. At the end of the ceremony my friend gave me a thumbs up and winked. It was at that moment I realized that the main reason I was nervous wasn't because of my pending nuptials, but because I expected my brother to show up and be himself.

Unfortunately, I let my guard down. So did my friend. My brother showed up half-way through the reception, a bottle in a brown paper bag held tightly in one hand and a cigarette in the other. By this time most of the room was happily drunk and dancing to the hits of the eighties. It was probably one of the happiest moments of my life. That is, until my brother walked up to the stage where the DJ was spinning "Take On Me" and grabbed the microphone.

In a way, it was interesting to see sixty people all come to a complete stop at the same time. Everyone turned to face the stage as my brother tapped on the microphone and cleared his throat.

"Ladies and gentlemen," he slurred, his eyes bloodshot and glassy. "Just wanted to stop by and say a few words about the...happy couple."

A low murmur rippled through the room. I felt Tanya squeeze my hand and I took a step forward to stand between her and my brother.

"You see, people, I'm the groom's brother. In most cases, this means I'm supposed to be the best man. You know, throw the stag party, hold the ring, all that jazz. But not in this case. Oh, no. I wasn't deemed worthy enough to stand in my brother's marriage to his current skank."

That's when three of my friends stepped forward out of the crowd. I turned to Tanya and saw the tears on her face. I wiped one away with a thumb and she smiled at me. Two of her girlfriends came over and led her away.

"We'll take her in back and freshen up her makeup," one of them said.

I nodded and turned back to face the commotion at the front of the room. One of my friends was smart enough to walk around the back of the stage and unplug the microphone, rending my brother powerless. The other two each had one of my brother's arms and were trying to lead him to the door, but my brother wasn't having any of that. He was squirming and jerking, trying to break their grip. The empty bottle in the brown bag lay forgotten on the dance floor.

When he saw me walking over his face turned a deep shade of red. "What the hell is this? Is this how you treat family?"

"You realize you just crashed my wedding reception and insulted my wife, right?"

"Fuck you," he spat. "This wouldn't have happened if you'd just invited me, stupid shit. It's your fault."

"Seriously?" one of my buddies asked. "You're such an

asshole."

My brother tried to turn to confront this insult, but that allowed my other friend to twist his arm up behind his back and frog march him to the door. They got him outside and I don't know what happened after that. My brother didn't show back up and my buddies wouldn't tell me anything. My guess is that they roughed him up a bit.

However, I did hear from my father, who I also didn't invite. I was a terrible son, a worse brother, and they didn't want anything to do with me. I accepted that as a wedding gift from the two of them.

The funeral started five minutes late, but I didn't mind. My body had adjusted to the cold, damp shirt under my coat, and I was fairly certain I could feel the pneumonia incubating in my chest. I tried to distract myself by focusing on the minister standing at the podium. He was a much older man, which fit in with most of the other people in attendance, and his wispy white hair framed his pale, wrinkled face, making him look like a cut-rate Einstein. He tapped the microphone a few times, thanked everyone for coming, then began the eulogy.

It was short and to the point, which was fine. I muffled a few sneezes and half-listened to the minister. He spoke the usual homilies, about the joys of fatherhood, of being a good person, a good Christian. He talked about the trials and tribulations of life and that it takes a strong person to make it through unscathed. None of it applied to my old man.

At one point I caught myself staring at the back of my brother's head. I wondered if he could feel me watching him. I could see him fidgeting, but that could have been from the cold chairs, or maybe he was craving a drink.

After a bit, the minister finished and asked if anyone would like to say a few words about my old man. The only sound was the cold air blowing through the vents in the ceiling. Most of the people in attendance kept their heads bowed. A few looked around. One couple stood, but once they entered the center aisle they turned to the back of the room and shuffled out. They didn't look at me as they left. I expected my brother to stand and speak. I assumed he had remained close to our old man, but maybe he was too shook up, or too drunk, to go through with it. The minister continued to wait, his face a neutral mask. He was probably used to scenes like this and had learned how to roll with it.

It seemed like five, maybe ten minutes passed before he gave up and asked everyone to bow their heads for a prayer. I bowed my head out of habit. I didn't have much use for religion, but some things are ingrained in a person when they're young and the habits are hard to break.

There was a group, "amen", then everyone stood and began to exit. I slipped out with the first few people. As soon as I passed through the front doors my eyes were seared by the bright sun and my chilled clothes actually felt good in the August heat. I fumbled in my coat pocket for my sunglasses as the group of mourners stood in a rough circle in a patch of shade thrown by the building. An official-looking man came outside and asked us to follow him to the graveside. The group turned to follow him and I watched my brother join the group. I hung back and waited for a few moments. This was going to be the final farewell and I wasn't sure if I was ready.

There was a time back when I was younger, probably around ten or eleven, when my brother and I had one of our first big fights. It was late summer, a few weeks before school started back up, and our old man was at work. My brother was supposed to be watching me, but he was too interested in just about anything else. I was in the living room playing Legend of Zelda on a second-hand console. I'd been playing all summer, preferring to stay in the relatively cool house instead of spending my time outdoors in what was being called the hottest summer on record. After weeks of making my way through the game I was nearing the end. All my focus was on the television screen, my fingers working instinctively on the controller. I didn't hear my brother come in from outside, the slam of the front door, his footsteps coming up behind me.

I don't know how long he was standing there. He may have said my name, but I was too caught up in my game to notice. I wanted to beat the game before school started. I was the only one of my friends who hadn't finished it yet. It was like being the only one who hadn't lost his virginity yet (not that I was even considering it at that age).

It was the faint smell of alcohol that got my attention. At that time my brother's drink of choice was whiskey, and the fumes seemed to exude from him on a daily basis. The smell slowly seeped into my brain and I felt my stomach tighten. I think my brain was aware of what was coming before I realized it. I flinched a moment before his hand smacked into the side of my head, which softened the blow. I rolled to the side and my brother stepped forward, stomping down on the gaming console. The image on the screen went haywire, then froze.

"What the hell?" I yelled as I got to my feet.

"Stupid shit," my brother slurred. "You just sit around all day playing your stupid games. Why don't you just...do something."

"Like get drunk?" I asked.

That seemed to throw him off balance. He looked down at the broken gaming console and kicked it. Pieces of plastic broke off and slid under the television stand.

"I was almost finished. Why did you do that?" My eyes were stinging from the tears that were welling up, and I was getting mad at myself for letting him see me get upset.

"Why?" He turned to face me. "Because. Because I don't like you. Nobody likes you. You fucked up everything."

"What are you talking about?" I asked, wiping at my face with the back of my hand.

"Everything was fine before you. I was happy. Dad was happy. Mom was alive. You're the reason everything changed." He punctuated the last statement by punching me in the chest.

I fell backward onto the couch gasping for breath. My brother didn't give me a chance to catch it. He fell on top of me and continued swinging. I deflected most of the blows by flailing my arms around, but he was bigger and faster and had the tenacity of a drunk. His fists found my face now and again, striking my cheeks, my eyes, the sides of my head. I could taste copper from a busted lip. Tears and snot mingled on my skin and I screamed before I lost consciousness.

I don't know how long I was out. My brother never told me. I came to in the basement, laying on the cold concrete floor. My nose was stuffed up and everything above my shoulders hurt like hell. I was trying to climb to my feet when the door at the top of the stairs opened and I saw my old man silhouetted in the frame.

"What the hell happened?" he yelled.

I was about to reply when I heard my brother's voice.

"We were playing hide and seek. He must have fallen down the stairs."

"Stupid son of a bitch," my old man grumbled. "Get him up here and clean him up."

My brother stomped down the stairs and grabbed the collar of my shirt to hoist me to my feet. He half carried, half dragged me up the stairs and into the bathroom.

"Here," he said, tossing a towel at me. "Clean yourself up."

The graveside ceremony was shorter than the service inside, which was a good thing. The crowd standing around the coffin were fanning themselves and wiping their faces so much I was wondering if we'd end up having to dig another couple of holes. The pastor or minister concluded by tossing a handful of dirt on the coffin lid, crossed himself, then stepped aside and began removing his coat and tie. An assistant pushed a button on a small controller connected to the platform that held the coffin. A small motor hummed and the remains of my old man disappeared into the earth.

The mourners stood around for a few minutes, either praying or waiting on someone who was, then they began to disperse. After a few minutes there were only two of us standing next to the grave. My brother wasn't looking at me. At least, I didn't think he was. I couldn't see past his sunglasses and he had his head bowed forward. I was hoping to be alone, to think my final thoughts about the old man, to, I don't know, maybe purge some of the bad crap that had built up inside me over the years. I couldn't say it to the old man's face, but I at least wanted to find some sort of closure. Maybe if I waited long enough my brother would wander off and I could have my time.

But instead he reached inside his coat and pulled out a silver flask. He took a long drink, screwed the lid back on, then tucked it back in his coat. At this point I was giving up and figured I'd head back to my car, crank up the air conditioning, then call Tanya. I'm sure she was wondering how things went.

"You're probably glad he's gone."

I looked up to see my brother staring at me. He'd removed his shades and his bloodshot eyes glared at me across the open grave.

"Glad? No." I replied. "More like relieved."

"Asshole. You're not even grateful for everything he did for you. He busted his ass to give us everything he could, and yet here you are dancing on his grave."

"I wouldn't call this dancing," I replied, pointing at my non-dancing feet. "Maybe it would be best if we didn't say anything and just..."

"You're ungrateful," my brother slurred, taking a few steps around the foot of the grave. "You killed both our parents and now you're a happy little bitch, aren't you?"

"What the hell are you talking about? Mom died from complications during surgery. Dad died from cancer. How the fuck is any of that my fault?"

"Mom died because of you. If you hadn't come along she'd still be here. She had that surgery because of you, so she wouldn't get pregnant again. That's on you."

I took a few steps towards him, sweat running into my eyes and making them sting, my head pounding in rhythm with my heart.

"So let me get this straight. Mom gets pregnant, has me, then five years later decides to have a hysterectomy and dies. That's my fault? How fucked up are you?"

"Dad blamed you, too," he replied, pulling the flask out again for another round. "He told me he blamed you."

I felt like I had been punched in the chest again.

"That...well, that explains a lot," I said. I think I'd known that all along, but never admitted it. Hearing the words out in the open was difficult, but good. It was like ripping off a bandage to find the wound beneath had healed.

We stood there in silence staring at one another. After a few minutes, I sighed.

"There's nothing left to say. Have a good life," I said as I turned to go.

My brother took a step forward and grabbed my shoulder, spinning me back to face him, then poked me in the chest with an index finger. "Oh, I still have something to say to you."

I pushed his hand away, but that's when he took a swing at me with his other hand. Luckily, he was half in the bag and I was sober, so I dodged it. He tried another swing that I ducked. I flashed back to my childhood, to that beating he gave me, waking up in the cold basement.

I didn't realize that I'd made a fist, that I'd swung it at him. It was the actual impact that got my attention, my fist striking him in the jaw. I saw his eyes roll back in slow motion, his head snapped back, arms out as he fell backward into the grave, the solid thump as he landed on top of the old man's coffin.

My hand hurt like hell, but I shook it off and stepped forward to look down in the hole. My brother was out, laying on his back, flask still grasped firmly in his hand. It was the perfect way to remember him.

I don't know how long I stood there, looking down at them. The cemetery was empty. Someone would be back later to fill in the dirt, but for now it was just the three of us. I thought back on my life with them. With my brother's admission fresh in my mind I reconsidered everything that had happened between us. I remembered all the snide comments, the bullying, the mean pranks, but now I saw them in a different light. I also thought about my old man and our relationship, or lack of one. Knowing how he really felt about me put it all in a new light. I had always thought he was just gruff, mean, an asshole. But it was more than that. He really felt spite for me, probably even hated me.

I didn't cry, although the emotions were there to set it off. Instead, I felt a sense of relief, of clarity. It felt as if at this very moment I was starting a new chapter of my life, burying the old.

There was a pile of dirt a few yards away, covered in fake turf. I pulled the covering aside and picked up the shovel that lay beside the pile. It was an old shovel, the wood handle smooth and polished from years of use. I dug the end into the pile of dirt, hefted it up, then turned and poured it into the hole. Then another, and another. I stopped to remove my coat and toss it over the headstone, then continued shoveling.

It must have taken me an hour to finish, but once I was done I leaned the shovel against the headstone and picked up my coat. My past was dead and buried. It was time to move on.

RESTORATION

It was three a.m. and the streets were empty. Simon cast one last glance up and down the sidewalk before shutting off the red neon "Tattoo" sign in the window. Business had been slower than usual over the past few days, but that was to be expected. It was Spring Break and most of the college students had skipped town to party at the coast. He didn't mind too much. It offered him a chance to take a breather from dealing with the usual drunk frat boys that stumbled in after closing time. The change of pace would do him good.

With the sign off and door locked, Simon returned to his work area to clean up. He had just begun dismantling the tattoo machines when he heard a knock on the door. Looking up, he saw a middle-aged man in a dark suit smiling at him through the glass. The smile reminded Simon of a barracuda. The man motioned for him to come unlock the door and Simon obliged.

"I've heard on the street that you're pretty good with a needle," the man said as he entered the parlor. The fluorescent lights reflected off his slicked-back hair, and Simon noticed the manicured fingernails. He knew immediately that this guy was a professional criminal, the kind that was usually well-connected. The man walked over to one wall and began admiring photos of Simon's handiwork.

Simon shrugged. "Yeah, well, I've been around for a while. You got something particular in mind?"

"As a matter of fact, I do," the man said as he turned to face

Simon with his toothy smile. He motioned to the wall with his thumb. "Nice stuff you've done, although I'm sure the photos don't do them justice."

"Look, I appreciate the compliments, mister...?" Simon trailed off.

"Brown. Just call me Mr. Brown."

"Okay, fine. Brown it is. Now is there something I can do for you, or do you just like to wander around tattoo parlors in the middle of the night?"

Brown's smile faltered for just a moment. "My apologies... Simon, am I right? Anyway, yes, I do have something in mind, but it isn't for me. I hear it's possible to do reconstructive work on tattoos...re-inking and restoring. Word on the street is that you're the best tattoo artist in the city, so would you be interested?"

Simon shrugged. "I guess I have a knack for it. But to be honest with you, man, I don't know. Restoring tattoos is a pain in the ass, and besides, it's getting to be four in the morning and I'm beat. There's probably two or three other guys in town who could help you out."

Again, Brown's smile faded, then quickly returned. "I'm not interested in any of the other guys. If it makes any difference to you, I'm willing to pay very well for your trouble."

"Like I said," Simon replied, "I don't..."

"How about five thousand dollars."

Simon almost choked. He leaned against the backside of a chair and ran his fingers through his hair. "I'd, ah, need to see the tattoo before I could accept. You know, to see how large an area I'd be working on, how detailed it is, stuff like that."

"Oh, it isn't too big," Brown replied. "It's on the left thigh, about the size of a softball. No color, either. And as far as detail is concerned, well, I think it's an old prison tattoo, so I don't think you'll have to worry about it being too intricate. But I can't let you see it before you make your decision. There are certain... extenuating circumstances and you have to be very discrete. Tell you what, would ten thousand dollars be enough to persuade you?"

"Can you give me a minute to think about this?" Simon asked.

Brown looked at his watch and nodded. "You've got five minutes."

Simon walked to the cramped office at the back of his shop and shook a cigarette from the pack on his coffee-stained desk. He couldn't get over the fact that this guy was willing to pay him that much money to fix up an old tattoo. The thing that worried him was that Brown was no small-time hood. He was obviously connected to the big leaguers, the guys who can make a person disappear without even breaking a sweat.

He took a drag off his cigarette and blew smoke at the yellowed bulb hanging from the ceiling. There was no way he could turn down this kind of money. Ten grand would solve most of his problems. But he couldn't shake the feeling that it seemed too easy, like a set-up. He snubbed the rest of his smoke in the ashtray and took a deep breath. It had been awhile since he'd taken a chance on something and this opportunity could pay off in a big way.

Simon returned to the front of the shop and found Brown talking on a cell phone, but he cut his conversation short before Simon could hear what was being said.

"So, have you made up your mind?"

"Yeah," Simon nodded. "I'll do the job."

Brown grinned. "Excellent. Are you ready to get started?"

"What, tonight?"

Brown reached into his jacket and pulled out an envelope. "Yes, tonight. Here. A down payment."

Simon opened the envelope. It was filled with cash.

"How much..."

"It's one thousand dollars, the standard ten-percent down, but I expect you to be worth it. You'll get the rest when the job is finished. I'll be back in a moment."

Brown turned and walked outside to the car waiting at the curb, leaving Simon standing alone in his shop with cash in hand.

Five minutes later Brown returned with another man. Between them they carried a large bundle wrapped in a sheet. Brown's companion was thick and bulky, the kind of guy that generally worked the door at a biker bar, although this guy looked to be classier. Like Brown, he wore a dark, tailored suit and his short cropped hair glistened with gel. Both men struggled under the weight of the package they carried as they shuffled across the room to the nearest table.

"Who's your friend?" Simon asked.

"An associate of mine. His name is Charlie and he will be supervising your progress tonight," Brown replied as he and Charlie heaved their burden onto the table. "Is everything ready?"

Simon nodded, but he couldn't shake the queasy feeling that was knotting up his stomach.

"Yeah, just tell Charlie to show me where…"

"He's not the one you'll be working on," Brown said with a laugh. With a wink at Simon, he turned and motioned for Charlie to open the sheet.

"What the fuck?" Simon said with a hitch in his throat.

The sheet was pulled back to reveal a body. It remained motionless on the table as Simon slowly approached.

"Now you can see why I needed your confidence," Brown explained. "The individual you will be working on met with an unfortunate accident yesterday morning. And sadly, it was before he had settled his affairs with us."

"This guy is dead," Simon whispered. His eyes were fixed upon the bullet hole in the man's chest.

"Quite right, Simon. It would probably be best if you could finish this up as quickly as possible. Decomposition will obviously hamper your efforts, so I suggest we turn down the air conditioning and…"

"Wait a minute," Simon said as he took several steps back from the table. "You want me to work on a dead body?"

Brown grabbed Simon by the shoulder.

"We have an agreement, Simon. Don't forget that. Charlie will remain here while I attend to some business elsewhere. If you need anything, like food or cigarettes, he will be more than happy to oblige. Are you ready to begin?"

Simon nodded, but he was barely aware of doing it. He felt like he was walking in a dream, disconnected from his body and merely along for the ride. The only thing he could think of was survival. Do the job, get paid, and forget that this night ever happened.

"Fine," Brown said, then nodded to his companion. "Take good care of this guy. I should be back in about an hour or so. Call me if anything comes up."

"Sure thing," Charlie replied as he settled himself into a chair near the far wall.

Simon rubbed a stubbled cheek with his hand, then stepped closer to the table to look at the dead body. The guy was about forty-five, maybe fifty years old. The hair on his nude body was gray and the skin was covered in a variety of tattoos. Most were done in blue ink, meaning they were probably done in prison. The only ink available behind bars comes in the pens they give you to write home with.

The dead man's face was a mass of wrinkles and the remnants of several bruises adorned his features. Something occurred to Simon and he leaned in for a closer look. The man was familiar, perhaps a previous customer. Simon shook his head and pulled up a chair.

Once seated, he began to examine the tattoo on the man's thigh. It was roughly a four by four pattern, blue ink. Definitely an amateur job. As he looked closer, Simon had a moment of déjà vu. Something about the design was familiar, but like the dead man's face, he couldn't place where he'd seen it before. Some of the more prominent features could still be made out, although most of the lines had run together. That was usually the result when the tat was done with a paper clip. It was going to be tough to fix.

"I'm not sure how much of this I can restore," Simon said. "Maybe if I had a better idea of what it was, you know? Like a picture I could work off of or something like that."

Charlie shifted his bulk in the chair. "Yeah, you see, that's one of the issues me and Mr. Brown been having. This guy is a former associate, sort of a runner, and he made off with one of his deliveries about eight years ago. He hid out for a couple of weeks, then got popped on an armed robbery, holding up a convenience store for a couple of microwave burritos. Can you believe that shit?"

Simon smiled, but he had stopped listening. His eyes were fixed on the tattoo as he remembered where he had seen the dead man before. His name was Ralph Monroe and he was Simon's cellmate at Starke eight years ago. Simon had been doing six months for bad checks, second offense, and had shared a cell with Ralph for two of them. They had traded stories, although Ralph had never mentioned Mr. Brown or Charlie while Simon had practiced tattooing on his companion's leathered skin. He even did a special request once, a map. Simon didn't think much of it at the time, but it obviously meant something to a few other people. When he got an early release he told Ralph to come visit some time. This wasn't exactly what he had expected.

"Couldn't you guys have gotten to him in prison?" Simon asked.

"Well, we didn't want word to get out that there was a shit-load of money laying about somewhere, you know? Too many greedy sons-a-bitches would be looking for it. Mr. Brown decided to wait until this guy got out. He figured the guy'd lead us right to it."

"Oh, so the tattoo is a map," Simon said.

Charlie nodded. "Yeah, some guy did it for him at Starke. He wasn't known for having the best of memories, and with this much money at stake he didn't wanna take any chances." He stood up and crossed the room. When he reached the table, he pulled a folded paper from his pocket and handed it to Simon.

"What's this?"

"A map. Mr. Brown circled an area in red. That's where he thinks the money is buried."

Simon unfolded the paper and found the spot marked by red ink. It was south of town, down in the Apalachicola National Forest, a place Simon knew fairly well. He had grown up in Tallahassee and spent most of his free time as a kid running around down there. That was after his father had left and before his mother had died, a time when he still had dreams of being a professional scuba diver. He used to dream about searching forgotten wrecks and undiscovered caves. Unfortunately, he lived too far from the coast to get any proper training, so instead he'd swim and dive in any available water hole he could find.

The forest near where he grew up was littered with sinkholes, and while there were quite a few areas open to the public, there was probably twice as much that remained relatively unexplored. A man could easily bury treasure out there and it would never be found. For all of Ralph's faults, he did have a few good ideas.

On closer inspection, Simon realized that he would have to look for a few good landmarks that corresponded with the tattoo. If he could manage that, then it wouldn't be too difficult to fill in the blanks and figure out the exact spot where the money was buried.

"I should probably get started," Simon said.

Charlie gave him a thumbs-up and returned to his chair. Simon opened a bottle of ink, slipped on his latex gloves, then took a deep breath and wondered what he had gotten himself into. He had run in some bad circles before, but most of those guys were petty criminals, small-time thieves and scam artists. Those days were far behind him. Over the last few years the worst he had to deal with were the frat boys with money to burn. Mr. Brown and Charlie were big-leaguers, professionals, and he knew that he was in over his head. He clicked on a lamp and brought it in closer to the faded design, then turned on the tattoo machine.

"You mind if I come over there and watch?"

Simon looked up.

"Yeah, sure. Just make sure you give me some elbow room."

Charlie dragged his chair over and sat near the end of the table, near Ralph's feet. As he sat down, Simon noticed a brief look of sadness cross Charlie's face.

"So you and this guy are old friends, eh?" Simon asked.

"Yeah, you could say that," Charlie replied. "Me and Ralph here go way back. Oh, I probably shouldn't have told you his name, huh? I guess it don't matter."

Simon dipped the needle in the ink, then began to trace the outside of the pattern.

"Too bad he had to run off with the money."

"It almost cost me...well, I was the one who recommended him. Mr. Brown hired him to deliver some merchandise, but Ralph never came back with the proceeds. Sixty-thousand dollars. Can you believe he'd run off with sixty grand? I mean, shit, he could've made twice that if he'd kept working for Mr. Brown for a few more years."

"Greed's a bitch," Simon mused. He dipped the needle and continued his work on the edge of the tattoo, doing his best to forget that he was working on a dead body. The skin was pale, ashen, and had a strange rubbery feel to it. At least he didn't have to deal with complaints about the pain.

He was just about finished with the perimeter, but the interior portion still worried him. It was a jumble of blurry lines and shapes, and he wondered what would happen if he couldn't complete the map. He also began to wonder what would happen if he did complete it. Honor among thieves was a product of the big screen. In real life, Simon knew just how easy it was get stabbed in the back.

"Speaking of money," Charlie said, "whatcha gonna do with that ten grand Mr. Brown is gonna pay you?"

"Well, I haven't given it much thought, but there's a couple of things I could do with it." Simon compared the map to the tattoo for a moment, then returned to his task. "The business here hasn't been exactly jumping lately and bills are piling up. Besides that, I've got an ex-wife down in Tampa who's been hounding me for alimony for the past year. The State started garnishing my income a couple weeks ago, so that's been hurting me as well."

"I figured as much. Mr. Brown said that you'd..."

Simon shut off the tattoo machine and looked up at Charlie.

"Mr. Brown said what?"

"Oh, nothing really," Charlie stammered. He reached into his coat pocket and pulled out a pack of cigarettes. "You mind if I smoke?"

Simon shook his head.

Charlie lit one up and blew a plume of smoke at the ceiling tiles. "Mr. Brown said something about you needing some cash. That's one of the reasons he picked you."

"What are the other reasons?"

"Well, he knew you had experience with prison tattoos," Charlie replied. "And he said something about you and Ralph being two peas in a pod. I don't know what that's supposed to mean, but I figured it meant that you'd know about maps and hiding shit."

Simon wondered if Brown knew that he and Ralph had been cellmates. It almost made sense. Find the guy that did the original tattoo. It wouldn't have been too difficult to figure out. When Brown realized that Simon was in need of money, well, that just made things a whole lot easier.

He laid the map next to the tattoo on Ralph's leg and began looking for landmarks. One spot appeared to be Silver Lake, just south-west of town. Simon filled it in, then began scanning for other familiar sites. Out of the corner of his eye he noticed that Charlie was losing interest in the restoration work and was looking around the shop. Finally, he got up and walked over to the far wall where Simon hung his work samples.

"So did it take you long to find this guy?" Simon asked.

Charlie dropped his cigarette on the carpet and ground it out with the toe of his patent leather shoe.

"Nah, not too long," he replied without turning around. "I mean, Ralph was good at hiding out, changing his identity and shit, but he slipped up. Mr. Brown did some checking and found out that Ralph had a great aunt or something that died here recently. He had a hunch that Ralph might head this way, you know? Here's this empty house that the dead aunt left behind, and we already figured that Ralph hid the money somewhere in North Florida, so we dropped in, found him home, and there you have it."

"Fascinating," Simon commented

Charlie turned and looked at his watch. "Mr. Brown will be back in about thirty minutes, so you'll need to wrap this up pretty soon."

"Sure, no problem," Simon replied as he stood up and stretched. "Just gimme about twenty more minutes."

He had just finished lighting up the cigarette he bummed off Charlie when Mr. Brown walked in the front door of the shop. The barracuda smile was back and shining brightly as he strode across the floor and patted Simon on the back.

"So I take it you've finished?" he asked.

Simon nodded and motioned at Ralph's body laying stiffly on the table across the room. "I'm pretty sure I know where your money is and I don't think you two will have any problem finding it. I took the liberty of marking it on the paper map Charlie gave me."

"Excellent," Brown murmured as he glanced over the map. "Charlie? Let's load up and get on the road. No sense in waiting around."

Charlie stood up and began covering up the dead man. "What about Simon?" he asked.

Brown scratched at his shadowy chin and looked at Simon for a long moment. "I think we'll take him with us. If he knows the area he'll probably come in handy."

"Wait a minute," Simon said. "This wasn't part of our deal. You said…"

"I know what I said," Brown said with a tight grin. "But sometimes things change."

Simon noticed that Brown's right hand had slipped inside the pocket of his suit coat. He nodded and took a nervous drag off his cigarette.

"Now, why don't you help Charlie with our friend over there and we can get going."

Grinding out his cigarette in the sink, Simon took a quick look at himself in the mirror hanging on the wall. His heart was beating heavy in his chest and his pulse was racing. He couldn't remember the last time he'd been this scared.

Little was said on the car ride south of Tallahassee. Simon rode in the front seat of the steel-gray Cadillac with Mr. Brown while Charlie sat in the back. Ralph had the trunk to himself. Except for directions, Simon remained silent, wrapped up in his own thoughts as civilization slipped away and the pavement turned into a wide dirt track. The forest stretched on for miles in every direction, with thick stands of pine and the occasional ancient live oak heavy with Spanish moss. Simon stared out the window and watched the scenery flicker by as his foot tapped nervously on the floorboard. The early morning sunlight was just beginning to break through the tops of the trees, causing a show of light and shadow against the brown and gray tree trunks.

Despite the situation, Simon felt a wave of nostalgia as they drove deeper into the trees. He tried to remember the last time he had been out here, but his memory was fuzzy and he could only guess that it had been at least ten years. It seemed as if very little had changed, if that was even possible. At least the roads had been maintained.

"Slow down here," he said as they rounded a curve. "You'll need to turn right up ahead."

Brown slowed the big car to a crawl and turned up a rutted track that disappeared deeper into the trees. Branches and undergrowth scrapped against the side of their vehicle like fingernails against a metal blackboard as it bumped along the winding path. After fifty yards or so, the car emerged into a clearing filled with scrub grass and exposed tree roots. It didn't look as if anyone had been out there for a while. Brown pulled the car over to one side, put the transmission in park, and turned off the engine.

"Okay, now where?" he asked.

"There," Simon replied, pointing to a sink hole a few yards away.

The three men got out of the car and walked to the edge. The sink was about forty yards wide, with steep sides sloping down to the water's edge. If Simon remembered correctly, the water itself was about twenty feet deep. There was a chain of sinks throughout the area, all connected by a series of underwater channels and tunnels. Quite a few people had drown trying to navigate them over the years, but Simon had been one of the lucky ones. He was one of the youngest cave divers in North Florida, although he had never been properly certified. Scratching his chin, he wondered if it was too late for him to get one of those certificates from the YMCA.

"So where the hell is my money," Brown asked, looking around the clearing with obvious annoyance.

"Take it easy, boss," Charlie commented. "Give the guy a minute to get his bearings." He poked Simon in the ribs with a beefy elbow.

"It's down there," Simon said as he pointed at the clear water.

"What? In the water?" Brown yelled. "How the fuck are we supposed to find it down there?"

Simon looked at Charlie, but didn't immediately reply. An idea was forming in his mind, a way to get out of this mess. He watched Brown stomp back and forth along the edge of the sink for a few minutes, then he cleared his throat and stepped forward.

"I can get it for you."

Brown stopped and spun on his heel. The toothy smile slowly reappeared on his face.

"Yes. Very good. You can get it," he said. He ran his fingers back through his hair and motioned for Charlie to come closer. "Throw him in."

Charlie looked at his boss, then shrugged and turned to Simon. "Sorry, buddy," he said as he grabbed hold of Simon's shirt and pants, lifted him a good two feet off the ground, and slung him out into the water.

It happened so fast that Simon didn't have time to protest or struggle. He flew awkwardly through the air and hit the icy water with a loud splash. The coolness of the water seemed to instantly clear his head, and as he broke the surface to catch his breath, he knew what he had to do.

Brown and Charlie were standing above him on the lip of the sink, guns drawn.

"No fucking around," Brown called to him. "Just find my money and this will all be over with."

Simon took a deep breath and dove under the water. The spring-fed water was crystal clear, and with the sun rising higher in the sky, it wasn't too difficult to navigate the shadowy bottom of the sink. There was quite a bit of debris and trash littering the sandy bottom, everything from beer cans and liquor bottles to air conditioning units and refrigerators. Simon slipped carefully among these items, his eyes scanning for anything that might hold sixty-thousand dollars in cash. As his lungs began to ache he saw it. A duffle bag was wedged under an outgrowth of roots, covered in slime and half buried in sand and rotting debris. He noted its position then surfaced to replenish his air.

"See anything yet?" Brown asked.

"Not yet," Simon replied as he wiped the water from his eyes. "It's pretty dark down there. Give me a couple more minutes."

Brown looked at his watch and nodded. "Fine, but you'd better hurry. I'm running out of patience."

Simon took a quick succession of shallow breaths, then one deep one before plunging back underwater. He kicked hard with his feet, propelling himself down to the spot where he'd seen the duffel bag. When he reached it he paused, glancing around to get his bearings. The duffel bag lay just outside the dark opening to one of the many tunnels connecting the sinks.

Grabbing the bag, he pulled it loose from the bottom and began dragging it into the narrow opening in the side of the sink. It was heavier than he expected and he expended most of his air getting it positioned in the tunnel entrance. His lungs were once again beginning to ache and his blood was pounding in his ears. In frustration, he shoved the bag aside and swam to the surface. As soon as he came up he heard Brown call his name.

"What the hell are you doing down there?"

Simon looked up at the two men standing above him with guns in their hands. He'd had enough of this situation, and without responding, he took a deep breath and ducked back under the surface. As he swam downward he heard several loud pops. They were shooting at him, but he didn't bother to look back. He was too deep for the bullets to hit him, and besides, he didn't want to waste any energy.

His heart was racing with fear and apprehension as he struggled to drag the money-laden bag through the opening. It was wide enough for two people to swim side-by-side, but it was also pitch black and Simon worried that he might not be able to find his way. It had been too long since he last navigated this labyrinth, and back then he'd had the benefit of a dive mask, flashlight, and compass. Now he was swimming on instinct, trying his best to remain calm and think clearly as he felt his way along the limestone walls. The cold water wasn't helping him, either. It made his limbs feel heavy and sluggish, although he seemed to recall reading somewhere that cold water actually slowed down the respiratory system. Supposedly, it allowed people to go for longer periods of time without oxygen. He hoped it was true.

He had no idea how far he'd traveled, but Simon was afraid it wasn't far enough. Once again he felt the desperate need to take a breath, his lungs aching as he struggled to keep his mouth shut. Random images began to run through his head, memories of his childhood and all the joy and pain that went with it. He saw the faces of his parents, images of friends and lovers, the adventures he had experienced as well as the errors in judgment he'd made.

But there was no way to go back, no way to relive it, no way to restore things once they are broken.

Then suddenly he saw it, a grayness in the water up ahead. At first he that it was a hallucination or perhaps the fabled white light that people claim awaits at the end of our lives. But after a few blinks Simon decided it was real enough. With renewed energy, he fought to swim the last few yards and exit into the dimly lit water of another sinkhole.

Dropping the bag, he kicked hard off the bottom, propelling himself to the surface. He broke water, mouth agape to suck in the desperately needed air. It took a few moments to catch his breath, and Simon was content to tread water as relief warmed his body. Gazing upward, he could see the sun had risen higher in the sky and now it's light and heat were breaking through the uppermost branches of the trees.

Simon smiled and, taking another deep breath, dove back under to retrieve the duffel bag. It was still heavy, but without a sense of urgency weighing down on him, the bag seemed easier to tote. He pulled it up along the bank of the sink and drug it to the edge of the tree line. He could still hear shouts and an occasional pistol shot echoing among the trees, but he didn't feel any fear. Brown and his companion would be wondering where he'd gotten to, but it would take them a while to figure out what happened.

By then he knew he would be miles away, the tattoo parlor and everything else that existed in his past life forgotten and cast aside like the wet clothes he was wearing. It was time for him to take the opportunity he'd been given and start over. It wasn't every day that one got a second chance, and he was determined not to waste it.

STRANGERS

It was a cold autumn evening and I was sitting before the fire lost in thought when the door opened behind me. I turned to see who had come in and found myself looking at an old woman whom I did not recognize.

At first I was startled by her appearance. Her face was a mask of wrinkles and her eyes were cloudy like blue opals. She carried a parcel wrapped in brown paper and I heard the soft, dry sound as her bare skin brushed against its surface.

For a moment we were frozen in time, staring at one another across the dark and hazy room. She seemed to realize that my mind had been elsewhere and she smiled, showing off her toothless mouth, but in that moment I saw a spark flicker behind her eyes, stirring a memory from the dust of years gone by.

Her wrinkled features faded and I saw a young woman, like the same woman I had married so many years ago, and my heart quickened at the memory. In my mind she had walked out the door just hours before, bound for the market, yet in my bones it felt as if fifty years had passed. I hid my confusion by returning her smile, and once satisfied she continued into the next room.

I turned back to the fire to resume my thoughts, but I had lost the path I had been on. The face of the old woman would not leave my mind and I could not understand what had become of the young girl I had married.

I thought that I should confront the woman who was now busy making loud noises in the kitchen, ask her what she had done with my fair-haired and smooth skinned wife, but something in the back of my mind told me to stay awhile and wait.

I threw another log onto the fire and sat back in my chair to watch the fresh wood spit and sizzle. My anxiety began to subside as I watched the flames dance amid the ancient bricks. Watching the fire was a secret pleasure of ours. I felt a smile on my lips as I thought about all the evenings spent sitting before the hearth with my beautiful bride.

Soon the odor of the fire was overpowered by the smell of fish broiling in the other room. The old woman was cooking, I assumed for me, but I had no idea why. Maybe my wife had made arrangements for her to tend to me while she was away.

It warmed my heart to know she still took care of me, even after all these years. I relaxed a bit and waited for the woman to call me to dinner.

Eventually my wait ended as the woman brought the food to the table. When she saw me begin to rise she shuffled to my side, grasping my arm and leading me to the chair at the head of the table.

Once I was seated she filled my plate with fish and new potatoes, then covered them both with a light gravy. My wife must have told her this was my favorite meal, the dear girl. She probably thought that by doing so I would not miss her as much, but alas, it only made me ache for her even more and I wondered when I would see her again. I used my napkin to wipe the tears from my eyes, then picked up my fork and ate to her memory.

After the meal was finished the old woman led me back to my chair by the fire, then went to clean up the table. Later she drew a chair up beside me and held my hand, her leathery flesh felt alien yet so familiar. My first reaction was to pull away, but for some reason I did not, so we sat together and watched the flames dancing in the darkness.

I felt the weight of the darkness pressing heavy on my mind. The old woman held my hand, but when I looked over I saw her chin resting on her chest and her eyes were closed. I did not wake her since she had prepared such a wonderful meal for me.

The night continued and the fire burned low. Dark red embers pulsated and winked amid the piles of ash. A chill began to creep into the room as the heat abated. The woman seemed to feel the cool and stirred, looking about drunkenly for a moment while her senses returned.

When her eyes turned to me she smiled again, pushing back the creases on her face and re-igniting the spark behind her eyes. The intensity of her gaze made me uncomfortable and I looked back to the dying fire as she continued to watch me and squeezed my hand.

Eventually even the embers burned to dust, and as the night crept towards the dawn the old woman rose and helped me to my feet. Together we slowly made our way down the unlit hallway and into the bedroom where she helped me into my nightshirt.

A single candle burned on the dresser and as I walked by I glanced into the mirror hanging on the wall. The face that stared back at me was a stranger. If I had ever known that man he was now a forgotten dream, shriveled and used up. His wispy white hair floated about his face like a mist, his eyes were empty and sad.

As we looked at one another I saw a single tear slip down his cheek and I reached out to brush it away, but the woman had come up and taken my arm to lead me to bed. I was glad she was there because I felt weak and could barely make my way across the room.

The sheets were cold but the comforter was thick and would soon keep me warm. The woman pulled up a chair beside the bed and sat, a look of concern on her face as she stroked my hair back from my brow. I looked up into her watery blue eyes and saw pity. She gave me a half-hearted smile and kissed my forehead. With a sigh I closed my eyes and remembered the girl I had married so many years ago.

SOLDIER STORY

It was autumn. Tomas could tell by the color of the wheat in the fields, amber and gold stalks swaying in the cool evening breeze. He could smell the wood fire that was coming from the farmhouse at the bottom of the hill. Gray smoke drifted out of the stone chimney and dissipated into the reddish sky. The sun was beginning to sink low on the horizon and the shadows grew longer along the ground.

The farm was familiar to him, but he wasn't sure why. The small house, built of stone and wood, sat on a flat piece of land in a long valley. On the far side was the barn, weathered and faded, but still sturdy enough. As he watched, a young woman walked out of the barn carrying a pail of milk. He felt his heart warm as she walked across the barnyard, scattering chickens along the way. He could hear their clucking and smiled.

The serenity of the moment was interrupted by a low rumble in the distance. Tomas turned to look up the road. From his vantage point he could see around the bend and the cloud of dust being kicked up by heavy vehicles. The warmth in his heart quickly turned cold and he felt it coursing through his veins.

He turned back to look at the farm and saw that the young woman heard the sound, as well. She dropped the pail, spilling the warm milk into the dirt. The chickens hurried over to see what it was while she ran into the house. A few moments later she reappeared with another woman. She was older and wore a stained apron that she was using to wipe her hands. He wanted desperately to go down the hill to them, to warn them, but he couldn't move his feet. He was an observer, nothing more.

Soon, two large trucks pulled into the farmyard. He hadn't seen vehicles like these before. The front end was like the front end of a large truck, and while the rear was like a large, canvas-covered truck bed, there were tank treads where the back tires should be. The only thing he wasn't surprised by was the German Army insignia painted in black on the steel gray doors.

Both vehicles came to an abrupt stop in the farmyard as brown dust and black exhaust circled in the air around them. He could smell the diesel, like poison in the fresh country air. Tomas wrinkled his nose and pulled a handkerchief from his pocket and cover the lower half of his face.

The scene below felt familiar, as if he had once seen it in a dream. An official looking soldier climbed out of the passenger side of one of the trucks as two armed soldiers jumped out of the back and hurried to walk on either side of him. They approached the two women on the porch and words were exchanged. Tomas couldn't hear them over the rumble of the heavy engines, but he felt as if he knew what they were discussing. The women both looked aggravated, the older woman was waving her finger in the important soldier's face, her gray hair coming loose from the bun she'd tied it in, while the younger woman put her hands on her face and sobbed.

Tomas felt his blood pressure rising and he struggled to run down the hill, but still he was locked in place, his feet planted firmly on the dark, rich earth. After a few minutes, one of the soldiers was given an order and he strode into the farmhouse. At this point, the cries of the two women finally overwhelmed the sounds of the truck engines, and Tomas felt their pain. When the soldier returned, he had one hand wrapped around the arm of a young man. Tomas felt dizzy, as if he'd stood up too quickly on a hot day in the fields. He dropped to his knees and tried to take a few slow breaths to calm his nerves.

The young man was dressed in plain brown pants and a wrinkled white shirt. His brown hair was disheveled and his eyes wide, looking to the older woman as the soldier dragged him off the front porch. The important soldier bowed stiffly at the waist and tipped his hat before turning on his heel and striding away. The other soldier remained at the porch, his rifle held across his chest as a warning to the women.

Halfway across the yard, the young man began to struggle and almost broke free from the soldier's grasp. When the other soldier turned and hurried over to assist, the old woman ran back into the house. She reappeared with something gripped in her fist, the other hand held her skirt so she wouldn't trip over it. When the young man saw her approach he stopped struggling and their commander ordered them to stand down.

The old woman approached the young man with tears streaming down her face. She grabbed his hands and kissed them, then handed him something. Tomas was too far away to see what it was, but in his heart he knew. The young man took it and hugged the woman. He then turned and climbed into the back of the closest truck. The two soldiers climbed up behind him and the canvas flap was closed. A minute later, the diesel engines revved up in a cloud of black smoke, then turned and headed back up the road.

As the sun set in a brilliant display of red and gold, the two women stood in the farmyard holding each other. Tomas could hear their sobs as they were carried on the evening breeze.

Tomas awoke laying on his side staring at a gray cinderblock wall. He shivered under the threadbare blanket and curled himself up as tight as he could. It didn't help much. He had both hands pressed between his thighs, but the cold seemed to have gotten into his bones and his fingers ached. He pushed his face into his mildewy pillow but after a few minutes his nose began to ache from being pushed sideways. Rolling onto his back with a groan, he looked up at the cracked ceiling and wished he was still asleep.

His eyes followed the cracks and outlines of the missing pieces of plaster. He had the patterns memorized and over time he's watched it slowly change, like watching glaciers melt, he thought. If he didn't think about it too hard, he could see shapes in the lines, animals and human faces. Some of them seemed familiar, people he had known long ago in another life, but he couldn't remember where or when. They were nameless shadows.

After a while he needed to relieve himself. He took a deep breath of stale air and hoisted himself off the thin mattress. The rusted springs underneath squeaked like a pack of angry cats as he stood. He limped to the toilet in the corner of the room, lowered his pants, and let out a sigh as his stream struck the porcelain. As he stood there he glanced at the nearby mirror and saw his wrinkled face and the remaining wisps of white hair that still clung to his scalp. Much like the cracks in the ceiling, the changes were slow to happen, but he knew every crease and crevice. However, instead of the cracks making a face, here the face made the cracks.

He shook the last few drops out, pulled up his pants, then limped back to his bed, climbing in and tucking his cold feet back under the blanket. A moment later he was sitting upright as he heard a knock on his door. It swung open to reveal a pretty nurse. She was his favorite. Her blonde hair was tied up in a tight bun on top of her head, her red lips parted in a sincere smile. She spoke quickly and clearly, but he couldn't understand a word. Over time he has been able to figure out what certain sounds implied. One sound she made meant pills. Another meant food.

The nurse kept up a steady stream of patter as she set the steel tray down on his nightstand, then turned to fluff up his pillow and prop it behind him so he wouldn't have to lean against the bare wall. He liked the sound of her voice. It was light, young, fresh, like listening to a mountain stream trickling through the forest. Listening to her made him forget the cold room and uncomfortable bed.

She handed him a small plastic cup with three colored pills inside along with a glass of water. He knew the routine. He tossed the pills into his mouth and washed them down with the chlorine-tasting water. She took the plastic cup and patted him on the shoulder. Next, she set the tray in his lap and pulled away the napkin that covered his bowl of oatmeal and a cup of black coffee. The tone of her voice seemed to indicate she was as disappointed in the usual breakfast fare as he was, so he nodded as if in agreement. She smiled and squeezed his hand, then turned on her heel and left the room.

He sat for a few minutes contemplating the cooling oatmeal while the smell of the coffee, acidic and earthy, made his stomach grumble. With a sigh, he picked up the spoon and began to eat. Not that he was that hungry, but he hated the sound of his stomach complaining.

Thinking about the nurse, he wished he could at least thank her for being so kind to him, much more so than some of the other staff, but he had learned his lesson long ago. Several of his bones still ached from those early days in the hospital, and his leg never did heal properly.

It was deep into winter and snow lay thick on the forest floor. Tomas sat high on the branch of a spruce tree, the heady smell of terpenes filling his nostrils. A clump of snow fell from the branch as he shifted his weight and it landed softly below. He looked about the almost silent forest and wondered why he didn't feel the cold.

He also wondered how he'd gotten here. The forest seemed familiar, but it was like a half-forgotten dream, wispy and hard to focus on. He took a deep breath of the cold air and exhaled. There was no sign of his breath in the air. Maybe he was a dream, or caught inside one. But the tree felt real. He could feel the bark of the spruce with his hands, feel the firmness of the branch under his butt, smell the piney smell of the woods all around him. Perhaps he would wake up in a moment.

After a few minutes of contemplation he heard the sound of voices and the crunch of footsteps breaking through the snow. An icy river gurgled roughly forty-five meters to the east of where he perched, and the sounds came from that direction.

Soon, a line of armed men appear, soldiers. Tomas can tell from the uniforms they are German Army. He somehow knows that the man in the front is a sergeant and aspires to join the SS. The others are conscripts, shoddily dressed in ill-fitting uniforms, most second-hand, complete with bullet holes and unpleasant stains. They shuffling through the knee-deep snow along the riverbank. They walk with their arms wrapped around themselves, scarves pulled up high on their faces. They don't march like seasoned veterans. They stumble and weave side to side like inexperienced recruits fresh off a farm.

As they reach an area mostly cleared of big trees, the gunfire begins. The rapid metallic popping of machine guns firing rips through the German soldier in the lead and takes out the two men behind him. The other soldiers, some splattered with fresh blood, jump into the snow and struggle to get their rifles off their shoulders. Once they do, the noise is deafening as the hidden machine-gunners and the German rifles unload at one another. Tree bark and spruce needles fill the air and mix with the smell of burning wood and gunpowder. The yells and screams of the men are drowned out by the noise of their weapons. Tomas, unable to close his eyes, covers his ears.

After what seems like hours, silence falls. The only sounds are the gurgling of the river and the soft groans of the injured. Tomas counts ten men who creep out from the cover of the big trees.

They are soldiers, too, but seem to be more in their element as they snowshoe to where their enemies lay dead or dying. Several pass close to him and he sees the insignia on their uniforms. They are Russian soldiers. He then realizes he is somewhere in Russian territory and feels a tightness in his chest.

He still isn't sure if this is a dream or not, so he remains on his perch hoping none of the soldiers look up his way. The Russians check the bodies of the German soldiers, confiscating anything of value and killing those who were still breathing. They laugh and trade some of the items they found, a watch for two packs of cigarettes, a pocket watch in exchange for a steel flask. Once they were satisfied, the men regrouped and strode back into the trees.

Tomas remained where he was, not sure if he should try to climb down or wait to see if he would wake up. He was almost ready to tempt fate and climb when he saw one of the dead Germans move. It was a body half submerged in the water. The Russians must not have noticed him. The previously dead soldier sat up, holding one hand against his bloody scalp, and pulled himself further up the bank. He lay there for a few minutes, then grabbed a handful of snow and held it against the left side of his head. It immediately turned crimson.

The soldier then got to his feet, swaying dangerously as he stumbled between his dead comrades. After verifying there were no survivors, he turned and began to follow the snowshoe tracks left by the Russians. From Tomas' vantage point, he could see the young man, soaking wet and still bleeding, walk between the tall spruce. A glimpse at the side of the soldier's face revealed him to be the same young man he saw at the farm and Tomas felt a shiver run through his body.

After several meters, the soldier stopped and knelt near a bush. Tomas scooted further down the branch to see better. The soldier had found a dead Russian left behind by his comrades. Tomas understood. The ground was too hard to dig a grave and the body too heavy to carry back to wherever their camp was, so they left him to nature. The injured soldier seemed to have another idea.

Tomas smiled as he saw the young man strip the uniform off the dead Russian and use it to replace his own soaking clothing. It wasn't a perfect fit. The dead Russian was much bigger than the young man, but that didn't matter as much as having dry, warm clothes.

The young man picked up another handful of snow to hold

against his head wound and continued into the forest.

The late morning sun felt good on Tomas' face. He sat in the hospital courtyard on a rickety wooden bench under the partial shade of an old, hoary oak tree. This was his usual haunt on warmer days. It felt good to breathe in the fresh air and feel the wind on his face. Sometimes he would sit here for an hour or longer, if the nurses allowed it, with his eyes closed and his mind at rest.

Today, however, he was busy with his hands. He was using a dull knife to whittle away at a piece of oak that had fallen near the bench two days ago. He had noticed it when he sat down. Over the course of the next hour he couldn't stop himself from looking back at it. It was the size of his forearm, yet probably stronger, he thought. There was something about it that caught his attention. Finally, he leaned over and picked it up, felt the weight of it in his hands, turning it over and over as if searching for something. He left it laying on the bench when he went back in for his lunch.

Later that afternoon he returned to the bench, sat down, then pulled a butter knife he'd stolen from the dining hall. With short, firm strokes, he ran the dull steel blade against the dried bark, at first removing splinters, then soon larger pieces. He worked methodically, stripping a few pieces on this side, then turning the branch to work on the other.

There was something inside the branch, an image, a shape, but he couldn't identify what it was. It was like seeing something out of the corner of his eye, but not being able to see it directly. So he worked cautiously so as not to damage whatever it was that was hiding from him inside this hunk of wood.

He was so intent on his task that he didn't notice when the blonde nurse stepped through the door accompanied by a young doctor. It was only after a few minutes that he felt that he was being watched and looked over his shoulder. When he saw the nurse he smiled and waved with the oak branch. The nurse smiled and waved back, then turned to say something to the doctor.

They were a few meters away, so Tomas could hear them talking in their secret language. Despite his inability to understand them, he could discern their tone. It seemed friendly enough and he wondered who this new doctor was. He had black hair, a smooth face, and his coat was white and free of wrinkles.

It made him think about his mother doing laundry. It had been many, many years since he had seen her. She did laundry at the river near their farm, at least during the warm months. He would often help her carry the baskets down the hill, then return to his chores until he heard her whistle for him to come help carry it all back to the house. His heart ached to think of her, so he pushed the memory aside and focused on the oak in his hands.

He felt like he had done this before, whittling away at pieces of wood, but it was somewhere in his forgotten past. Little flashes of memory, like gunfire, popped and faded in his mind. There was nothing tangible, just impressions of things he may or may not have done. The wood, however, felt like a missing connection, like there was something inside it that would help him to remember. He was sure of it.

His old, arthritic hands began to tremble and he dropped the knife. As he reached down for it, the nurse appeared at his side and picked it up. She held it in front of his face, her brow furrowed, and said something in a disapproving tone. Tomas bowed his head and wondered if she would give it back.

She was interrupted by the doctor. He walked over and took the butter knife from the nurse, examining it closely and running the pad of his thumb over the edge. He said something to the nurse, shrugged, and handed it back to her. She asked a question, the doctor nodded, so she gave the knife back to Tomas.

That was when Tomas decided he liked this new doctor.

Judging by the screams of pain and the people moving about in blood-stained white coats, he knew he was in a medical facility. Tomas entered one of the large canvas structures and walked between the rows of cots as if passing through a daydream. No one noticed him, the doctors and nurses, the patients, they all went about their business of experiencing pain and relieving pain as if he wasn't there.

Tomas walked towards the back of the makeshift hospital room and saw the young man from the river bank. He had to grab hold of an IV stand for support as his head swam for a moment. The young man had a pink-stained bandage wrapped around his head and appeared to be sleeping but his legs shifted and kicked beneath the gray blanket and he let out low moans. Tomas walked to the bedside and wondered if the young man remembered to retrieve the chess piece out of his pocket before switching uniforms with the dead Russian soldier.

With a bandage covering half his face, Tomas couldn't make out all the young man's features, but he felt his heart ache as he looked down on him. Dried blood still colored part of his exposed cheek and the side of his neck. What could be seen of his face was sunburned and covered in the beginnings of a sparse beard. Tomas smiled and reached down to lay his hand on the young man's head.

He was interrupted by a doctor and an orderly. They stood at the foot of the bed, the doctor looking at a clipboard with bloodshot eyes. He spoke to the orderly in that secret language Tomas couldn't understand. The doctor stepped to the other side of the bed and gently shook the young soldier until he awoke.

The young man's red-rimmed eyes opened a bit, then grew wide as he took in his surrounding. He tried to sit up, but the doctor's hand on his shoulder held him in place. After a moment he complied and his eyes flicked back and forth between the doctor and the orderly.

The doctor spoke, asking questions that had no meaning to either the young soldier or Tomas. He spoke again, more slowly this time, but still there was no recognition or response from the injured young man. Tomas felt bad for him. He knew what it was like not being able to understand the words of the people around him.

After several attempts, the doctor turned to the orderly and said something to the orderly. The other man nodded and hurried away, only to return a moment later with a second orderly and a stretcher. They got it positioned under the young soldier, then lifted him and carried him away.

Tomas followed them outside and watched them load the young soldier into the back of a panel van along with several other patients. They closed the rear doors and smacked their hand several times on the side of the vehicle. In response, the van revved its engine and pulled away.

He watched as its made its way down the muddy dirt road, bordered on either side by gray snow and slush. Within minutes, it had disappeared over a hill.

The cool days of spring were now growing warmer as the days passed. The piece of wood was still hiding its secret, but Tomas continued his painstaking work with the dull knife. He had hoped the nurse would take pity on his gnarled hands and give him a sharper instrument, but that hadn't happened yet. At least with this blade, it was so dull he really couldn't cut himself.

There were small wood shavings scattered around the bench and on top of his worn slippers. Each afternoon, Tomas would get up to go inside and determine the progress he had made by the size of the pile. In the late mornings when he'd return, the pile would be mostly gone, either blown away by the evening wind or picked up and carried away by birds or squirrels. It made him smile to think he was providing building supplies for a new nest.

Today he had to take off his jacket, but even then small beads of sweat were running down his forehead. He wiped his face with the back of his sleeve and turned the piece of wood over in his hands. Changing his perspective helped him to determine the next step. Although the knife he was using limited how much he could remove with each stroke, he wanted to work slowly, cautiously, so as not to remove too much. He knew he was getting closer to the hidden figure, it was only a few strokes away.

The touch of a hand on his shoulder made him flinch. Old habits were hard to break, unlike his bones. He turned his face up to see the golden-haired nurse smiling at him. He smiled back at her as his heartbeat began to return to normal, then he held up the piece of wood to show her his progress. The nurse's smiled widened and she nodded her head. Tomas felt the sweat begin to run down his face and returned to his task.

After a few minutes, the nurse tapped him on the shoulder again and spoke in her secret language. Tomas smiled back as he had learned to do, even though the nurse would never discipline him. She said something else, then took him by the hand and helped him to his feet. With one hand on his elbow and another holding his hand, she led him back towards the hospital. He hesitated, looking back at the piece of wood he'd left on the bench, but the nurse said something that, even though he couldn't understand her, made him relax. She would look after it, he thought to himself.

It took a few moments for his eyes to adjust to the interior lighting and he felt goosebumps rise on his damp skin. He suppressed a shiver as the nurse took him down the first-floor hallway, then through a frosted-glass door with strange writing on it.

The office wasn't much larger than his hospital room. A gray metal desk was near the far wall, and the buzzing fluorescent light was almost blinding as it reflected off the bare white walls. To his left was a long folding table covered in hardback books of various sizes and colors, stacks of papers, and some electronic devices. He had no idea what they were, but they appeared benign.

The nurse brought him to the paper-covered examination table against the other wall and helped him sit on it. She patted him on the knee and said something, then shook her head and gave his hand a squeeze before walking out and closing the door.

Tomas sighed and looked around. It was one of the doctor's offices, but he was surprised at the lack of clutter. Most of the doctors at the hospital had been there many years. He had seen dozens come and go during his stay, but over the past several years more had remained for longer periods. Once they were settled in, their offices would begin to accumulate more and more books and papers. Filing cabinets would take up most of the available wall space, and framed documents, usually crooked and dusty, would hang behind the desks.

But here was different. The paint on the walls smelled fresh. Tomas pressed a finger against it to see if it was still wet, but it wasn't. There were no frames on the walls, no filing cabinets, no clutter to speak of other than the items on the folding table.

He looked over when the door opened and the new doctor walked in as if he was late. The young man stepped around the desk and picked up a thick file folder from the desk. The file was heavy, the cover yellowed, stained, and taped together in several places. The doctor opened it up and began flipping through the pages, pausing every so often to read more on a specific page. Other than the buzz from the ceiling lights, the room was quiet.

The doctor finally looked up and asked Tomas something in the secret language. Tomas sat and smiled. The doctor frowned and repeated the unknown words. Tomas smiled and nodded, unsure of what the doctor wanted him to do. He kept smiling to hide how uncomfortable he felt. He remembered the questioning when he first arrived at the hospital, both in his mind and in his bones.

Tomas flinched as the doctor came around the desk and leaned against the front of it, his crossed arms holding the file against his chest. He frowned at Tomas' reaction and reopened the file. After several pages he stopped and began reading, shaking his head and mumbling under his breath. When he finished he set the file back on his desk and walked over to stand in front of Tomas.

Face to face, Tomas felt as if he should look away, but the doctor took both of Tomas' hands in his and said something.

Tomas shook his head, not knowing what he was supposed to do. The doctor said something else, different sounds, but still Tomas was confused. Again and again, the doctor made sounds that were different from the usual secret language everyone in the hospital used. Different tones, different inflections. Each time, Tomas shook his head until his eyes welled with tears.

The doctor stopped speaking and stared at the floor for a moment, then he looked up with a grin. He gave Tomas' hands a squeeze, then walked over to the folding table and rummaged through the papers. After a moment he pulled a folded paper from one of the stacks and began to unfold it on top of the cluttered tabletop. He looked back at Tomas and motioned for him to come over.

Tomas slipped off the exam table and shuffled over to join the doctor. Looking down, Tomas saw it was a map. His eyes roved over the document and he realized the characters he saw matched the ones on all the doors and signs in the hospital. More of the secret language.

The doctor pointed to both Tomas and himself, then pointed to a spot on the map. Tomas leaned in and nodded. He assumed the doctor meant this was where they were on the map. The doctor then traced his finger down one of the lines, then another, then another. Tomas watched, not understanding what the doctor was doing. Each time the young man traced one of the lines he said something, a secret word, but it was different for each one. When he realized Tomas didn't understand, he tried again using different words and tones. Tomas continued to scan the map, the land masses, the oceans.

Then his eyes grew wide. He realized he was looking at Europe. He remembered it from when he was a child, a map in his schoolroom showed the same view. He leaned in closer as the doctor stepped aside. Tomas ran a crooked finger around a familiar shape, a country that seemed very far from where the doctor indicated they were.

Tomas straightened up and looked at the doctor while pointing at the spot on the map. The doctor nodded, then retrieved a book from one of the stacks. He opened it and thumbed through it until he found what he was looking for. Setting it down on the table, he again stepped aside to allow Tomas a chance to look closely. It was the same country he had pointed to a moment ago, but this time it filled two pages in the book. There were more details, more landmarks like rivers, lakes, mountains. Even though he couldn't read the place names, they seemed familiar, familiar enough that Tomas felt tears welling up in his eyes.

His first few months at the hospital were a blur of pain and blood. Tomas stood in the corner of a room and watched as the doctors beat the young man strapped to the bed. The head wound had not yet healed and the violence had reopened the wound. Blood soaked into the thin pillow, the sheets, and formed a small puddle on the floor beside the bed.

Tomas wanted to run out of the room, but his legs wouldn't respond. Instead, he stood in the shadows as the doctors yelled at the young man in their secret language. They yelled into his face, the young man shook his head, and the doctors responded with slaps and punches.

Finally, the doctors took a break. The walked to a table near Tomas and one of them picked up a thin file folder. The two men reviewed the handful of documents inside, then had a brief discussion. Afterwards, one of them left the room while the other returned to the bedside. He took a towel from the nightstand and used it to wipe the blood from the side of the young man's face.

The other doctor returned with several other men. Tomas recognized them as orderlies, the men who assisted the doctors and moved the patients from room to room. They rolled in a gurney and positioned it next to the bed, then hoisted the young man like a rag doll. Tomas could hear him groaning as they rolled him out of the room.

He followed the group down the cold hallway. Muffled voices echoed behind closed doors like whispered memories. Tomas shuddered and wrapped his arms around himself. The men were walking much faster than his tired legs could move, and they soon entered a room at the end of the hallway. Tomas was too slow to slip into the room, but he saw them attaching the electrodes to the young man's head just before the door closed.

Tomas sat on the edge of his bed and examined the piece of wood, turning it to and fro as his eyes scanned every millimeter. He was almost there, the image was just behind a wispy veil. All he had to do was a few more careful strokes and it would be revealed.

But it wouldn't happen at the moment. The golden-haired nurse had made it very clear that he was not to whittle in his room. She was angry the last time he did it, and she made him clean up the wood shavings that were scattered across the bedsheets and floor. He made sure to find and dispose of every sliver.

He was supposed to be sitting on the bench by this time of the morning, but the nurse hadn't come to get him yet. Instead, he tried to sit quietly and wait for her, but he couldn't stop his hands from trembling. Being so close to his goal was exciting. This was the happiest he had been in a long time.

He twitched when the door opened and the nurse walked in, followed by the doctor and another man. The new person wasn't wearing the standard white coat that the other doctors wore, and he wasn't in the green outfit that identified the orderlies. Tomas stood and smiled while holding the piece of wood behind his back.

The nurse stood aside to allow the two men to enter, then stepped into the hallway to retrieve two wooden chairs. Once the men were seated, the nurse left and Tomas stood beside his bed unsure of what to do next. He watched as the men talked to each other in the secret language, then the doctor looked up and motioned for Tomas to sit. Tomas set the piece of wood on his nightstand and eased himself back on to the mattress.

The doctor spoke briefly to Tomas, paused, then said something to the man beside him. The man nodded, scooted his chair closer to the bed, then leaned in.

"Hello" he said.

Tomas felt the smile on his face freeze in place. He couldn't move. The man said something that he understood. He looked at the doctor, who was smiling, and then back to the stranger.

"Do. You. Understand. Me?" the stranger asked.

Tomas nodded, but it felt as if he was moving through molasses. He understood the words, but at the same time they seemed foreign, the accent different from what he was used to here in the hospital. He wanted to respond, but the words were difficult to form. He could see what he wanted to say, but the words wouldn't form on his lips.

The doctor and the stranger conferred for a moment in the secret language, then they turned back to Tomas.

"I. Am. Serge," the stranger said, his deep voice tingling in Tomas' ears. "Can you tell me your name?"

Tomas shook his head. He tried to move his mouth, to force the words to take shape, but it wouldn't obey. All that came out were half-formed sounds.

Serge patted Tomas' hand. "It is okay. I am here to help. You are from Hungary, correct?"

Again, Tomas nodded as tears began to run down his cheeks. He was no longer a stranger in a strange land.

Several weeks passed before Tomas was able to return to his bench in the garden. The excitement he'd felt for his whittling had been replaced by something more important. Discovery.

Serge worked with him every day, four hours in the morning, four hours in the afternoon, with breaks for lunch and dinner. Tomas was mentally exhausted every night, but by morning he was ready for more. Within days he learned that Serge was a speech therapist who had studied in Europe. The doctor had contacted him after reading through Tomas' file and showing him the map. Like a detective, the two men realized that Tomas was not a Russian soldier with a serious brain injury. He was a Hungarian farm boy who had been lost for over fifty years.

It took almost three weeks before Tomas regained the ability to converse in Hungarian at a child's level. It wasn't much, but it was progress. The fact that he could talk to someone else and understand what they said was a revelation to him. Decades of isolation had to be undone and it would take time to repair the damage.

After six weeks, Serge had to leave to attend to some other duties, but he promised Tomas he would return soon. The doctor, it turned out, had begun taking lessons in Hungarian in order to better treat Tomas. They both had a similar level of understanding, so they were able to communicate quite well.

Tomas was ready for a break from relearning his language, so he returned to the bench and sat in the noontime sun with his piece of wood and knife. There were fewer shavings under the bench and the piece of wood was reduced to the size of a misshapen fist. Tomas didn't realize that he was smiling.

With careful, graceful strokes, Tomas whittled away a few more strands, mere splinters, and finally reached his goal.

"It appears to be a horse, or at least a horse head" said a voice from behind him.

Tomas looked up to see the doctor, still smiling, and nodded his head.

That night, Tomas dreamed he was back on the farm. This time, instead of being on a hill, he was standing next to the young man as the old woman ran to him to say her goodbye. The smell of diesel exhaust from the German army vehicles was almost suffocating, but he stood quietly and watched.

The old woman, tears streaming down her cheeks, hugged the young man so tightly that Tomas could hear him gasp for breath. When she released him, she reached into her apron and pulled out something, stuffing it into the young man's hands before she turned away. The young man gripped it for a moment, then opened his hand.

Tomas saw the chess piece, the knight, that he had been whittling, the one he had lost at the riverside fifty years ago.

It was finally going to bring him home.

AFTERWORD

I always enjoy it when an author adds an afterword to their collections that gives some background and context to the stories. So I'll continue that tradition with this collection.

Reflections in Blue Water

I was inspired to write this after reading the short story, The Swimmer, by John Cheever. The story got me thinking about swimming, about pools, about wealth, about relationships. I was also reading a lot of Raymond Carver at the time, who also wrote many stories about relationships, alcoholism, depression, and blue-collar America.

With this story I just wanted to see if I could write something in the spirit of these two amazing authors. I think I did okay.

Compatibility

This story was inspired by a guy that worked in the same office as me several years ago. He wasn't someone I interacted with. In fact, not many people in our office spoke to him. He was ex-military, extremely loud and opinionated, and he fancied himself a "man's man". It wasn't unusual to hear him yelling at his wife over the phone during office hours. And he didn't seem to care what we heard.

I was talking to a coworker one day when this guy walked by full of bluster and bravado, and it occurred to me that it would be hilarious if he was actually a cross-dresser or something like that. I was tickled by the idea that someone who is overly manly actually hid a deep dark secret.

A few days later I wrote the first draft. The guy who inspired this story has long-since retired and now spends his free time writing angry letters to the editor of the local newspaper.

Dirty Laundry

Originally, this story was a screenplay I had written for a screenwriting course I attended. I went on a spree of reading nothing but scripts for a few weeks so I could understand how they were different from writing prose. They were nothing but dialogue and some stage direction. I found it fascinating how those pages could be interpreted by a director and turned into a film.

Fast forward a few months and I had an idea that seemed a good fit for my first attempt. It came to me while…wait for it…I was doing laundry in a laundromat. My washing machine had died so I had to find a bunch of quarters and carry my dirty unmentionables down to the local Suds-o-Rama (or some similar sounding name). Watching the employee that was working that night, along with the the eclectic handful of customers, sparked my imagination.

The screenplay turned out okay. I put it aside for about a year before picking it up again to see if I could do a better job. After a few more weeks of frustration, I gave up and decided to convert it into a short story. I'm much happier with it in this form.

Spring Mourning

I wrote this story about twenty-five years ago sitting in a library at Florida State University. I was jotting down story ideas while waiting for a friend and for some reason I started thinking about my late mother. My biological mother died when I was a wee lad and I never got to know her. In fact, I don't have any tangible memories of her.

I started thinking back to that time. One of my earliest memories is that of the wake at our house after the funeral. I remembered the crowd of people, all somber and dressed in black, and I remember being uncomfortable and not understanding what was going on.

And that was the catalyst for the story. That's me saying the goodbye I never got to say. It's a bit depressing, of course, but when I finished writing it I felt a sense of relief, of closure. It also felt like a good story. Simple, sweet, and a bit different from my usual weirdness.

A Game of Chess

So the background for this one is that I had been reading some short stories written by Gabriel Garcia Marquez and wanted to try something metaphorical and with a touch of magic realism. I'm not sure why I decided on chess as the game to be played, but it seemed to fit as a nice parallel to the seduction. In both cases there's strategy, proper positioning, and a bit of subterfuge.

For what it's worth, I didn't just make up the chess moves. In fact, I played several matches against a chess program on my PC. I then printed out the moves from the best match and used them in the story. So yes, it's actually based on an actual game of chess. The rest is completely made up.

Roids

I'm really not sure what sparked the idea for this story. I remember writing the opening scene and decided that the protagonist was buying hemorrhoid ointment. I wasn't sure where the story was going to go after the kidnapping, but then I realized that "roids" could mean hemorrhoids or it could mean steroids. After that epiphany the rest of the story came together in a two-hour writing spree.

But it does raise a serious question. What happened to Preparations A through G?

Last Rites

This one pulls from both my own personal history and that of an acquaintance. Except for the murder part. That was pure fiction.

I've said many times that all families are dysfunctional in their own, unique ways. With this story I wanted to explore that a bit. I wanted to show that just because people are related doesn't mean they are family and that emotional wounds can take a long time to heal.

When I started writing this one I didn't know how it was going to end. I felt that letting the protagonist's emotion carry me through would lead the story where it needed to go. I was startled a bit when I wrote the last few lines, but it felt like a satisfying conclusion.

Restoration

I had watched a fascinating documentary on prison tattoos several years ago and it stuck in my head. I started thinking about all the different tattoos, what they meant, and how the inmates figured out how to create this unique art with whatever tools were available.

Then I got to thinking, could the tattoos be used to convey a message, or maybe to remember something? Like buried treasure?

From there, the story took off on its own. I kept the setting local because I wanted to include the area. The national forest south of where I live is expansive and filled with sink holes and natural springs, a perfect place to hide something. And I don't see North Florida utilized very often.

Strangers

This is one of the older stories in this book. I wrote it after my maternal grandparents died. I hadn't seen them in years because they lived in England and I was in the US, and, well, plane tickets are expensive. But I had fond memories of them from when they lived here when I was younger and they always seemed to have a special relationship.

After they were gone, I felt like I wanted to write something about them. The characters here don't physically resemble my grandparents, at least not in my imagination, but I think the interactions are inspired by them. I like to think they'd be flattered.

Soldier Story

The inspiration for this story came from a news article I had read. The basics are similar to what happens in my story: a young man in German-occupied Europe is conscripted by the German army and forced to fight on the Eastern Front. He was later captured and, because he couldn't speak Russian or German, was sent to a sanatorium. Almost sixty years later, someone on staff at the hospital realizes what happened to this poor man and he is eventually sent back to his home country.

Truth is often stranger than fiction, so I took the premise and fleshed it out into something deeper. I wanted to go inside this man's head to understand what he'd been through, what he was thinking, and eventually, how he is finally able to return to the real world.

Sadly, I tried to find more information on what happened to him after he was repatriated, but I guess the media lost interest in him.

ABOUT THE AUTHOR

Richard Bist has been writing fiction for over twenty-five years. His work has been published in a variety of both print and online publications. He also hosts a creativity podcast, The Prometheus Project, and a cooking show on YouTube ingeniously titled, Richard's Kitchen.

He currently resides in North Florida where he spends his free time wrangling two mutts, cultivating carnivorous plants, and trying to catch up on the unread books on his nightstand.

For more information, please visit www.richardbist.com.

www.ingramcontent.com/pod-product-compliance
Lightning Source LLC
Chambersburg PA
CBHW070633130626
46555CB00006B/2537